# A Lady's Secret

## by

## Sarita Leone

*A Willowbrook Manor Romance,*
*Book Three*

**A Lady's Secret**

Cover Art by *Debbie Taylor*

The Wild Rose Press, Inc.
PO Box 708
Adams Basin, NY 14410-0708
Visit us at www.thewildrosepress.com

Publishing History
First Tea Rose Edition, 2016
Print ISBN 978-1-5092-0757-2
Digital ISBN 978-1-5092-0758-9

*A Willowbrook Manor Romance, Book Three*
Published in the United States of America

**Amy cringed.**

Even the knock on the door sounded angry. "That will be Oliver." Will looked from wife to friend, then shrugged. "If I do not open the door, I suspect he will knock it in."

"Let him in, dear." Vivian sat beside her on the small settee and now patted her hand. "We shall talk some more, but I think now we are ready to face the rest of this lovely day, aren't we?"

They had been that way for hours, holding hands and sharing confidences. Well, Amy had shared mostly, both confessions and a multitude of tears. She had not gotten any harsh judgment from Vivian, only soothing words of encouragement and many back rubs. It had been just what she needed most, a caring ear to listen and other shoulders to help carry the burden of her secret.

She scrubbed her palms over her cheeks, praying the evidence of her tears had not turned her ugly. A Friday-faced female never garnered a man's good attentions, and she did not wish to be seen in such an unflattering light.

"Yes, I do believe we are." When Will turned and went to the door, she reached out and pulled Vivian into a quick embrace. Whispering into the other woman's ear, she said, "Thank you. I feel ever so much better now."

# Dedication

Always, for my sweet man.

Chapter 1

*London, 1816*

Being a peer had its advantages. Lord Oliver Gregory was accustomed to getting what he wanted, when he wanted it. Being kept waiting sent his genial nature upside down. He turned to his assistant with a scowl that would have cowed a lesser man.

"We can't just stand here like a pair of lamp posts. Dash it all, we've got to do something."

Will Fulbright had been through too many difficult times with his employer to be put off by a facial expression. He kept his tone neutral when he spoke.

"What would you have me do, Your Lordship?"

"Don't call me that, for one thing." Oliver kept his gaze fixed. "Especially here. I would rather my presence go unnoticed."

He stared at the wooden black door set discreetly into the façade of the building directly opposite. No sign of anyone entering or exiting. To passersby, the three-story brick edifice would not bring attention. It was like so many others in the city, flat-fronted, weathered red-brick, complete with black shutters on the ground-floor windows to keep prying eyes from…well, from prying.

But Oliver knew better. He was aware of what the ordinary exterior concealed. And, he and Will had witnessed, barely fifteen minutes earlier, a parlor maid from his own estate slipping inside. Had Bridget not been one of his mother's favorites, he would simply have terminated the young woman's position at Willowbrook Manor. But she had been with the family for quite some time. Therefore, he could not dismiss her without attempting to question the woman. As well, Bridget's sister was his own sister Lucie's lady's maid. Upsetting Lucie's maid meant upsetting Lucie—and that was something to be avoided entirely.

"Then perhaps we should leave." Will turned to take a step toward the corner, and undoubtedly would have turned onto the next lane without taking a single look back, but Oliver grabbed a fistful of gray morning coat and gave it a tug.

"We are not leaving until we have rousted that woman from that-that…" Oliver's lips snapped closed in disgust. "From that place, that—"

"Whore's den?"

"Good Lord, man—have you no shame?"

Oliver glanced over his shoulder, but no one seemed to pay them any mind. Apparently two well-dressed gentlemen standing in the shadow of one building while staring at another wasn't enough to warrant curiosity.

"I haven't done a thing to be ashamed of. Let me point out the obvious—you haven't done anything, either."

"Not today. But have you forgotten my past?" Oliver was never going to be proud of, nor forget, what had taken place earlier in his life. And although it had been two years, give or take a month or so, since he had returned from abroad a raving lunatic, the memories were never far from his mind.

"I have not forgotten, although I do believe it would serve you better if you did attempt to let the events settle back in your head, into the fuzzy, out-of-focus spot reserved for escapades of that sort."

"Never." Oliver would not allow time to dull his accountability. He had nearly ruined his family and caused his own demise. No, time should not be allowed to cast his failings in a favorable or even fuzzy light. He shifted his weight from one foot to the other. His boots felt tight around the ankle he had twisted last week during a riding accident.

"Your ankle still pains you." Will pointed with his walking stick to the swollen area. "It bulges against the leather. We may have to cut you out of those. Come on, let's get going. We cannot wait here all day. She may never come out."

Oliver ground his molars so hard a pain shot up his cheek. Taking a deep breath, he forced himself to unclench his jaw. He hadn't wanted to be pushed into this position, but it seemed there was no other way.

He would have rather ridden post haste to Gretna Green with the least attractive woman in his social circle—a sudden image of one gap-toothed, frizzy-haired daughter of an earl who had feet long enough to paddle a boat filled his head—than enter a den of iniquity. But the earl's daughter was not at hand, and the maid needed saving, so he squared his shoulders.

"Correct. She may never come out—and that is precisely why we are going in. We shall retrieve Bridget and be on our way. Now, let's go."

"But-but—Oliver, are you sure about this?"

The fact that his assistant not only used his

Christian name but did so at a rather high volume right in the center of Bond Street—for Will had followed on his heels the moment he moved from the shadows toward their destination—showed just how unwise going into such an establishment could prove to be.

One temptation not ignored had the potential to pull him back into the horror he'd worked to leave behind. That is all it will take, Oliver thought. Bile rose in his throat, but he swallowed it down. He did not plan to fall under the spell of any demon that had held him captive prior.

He would just go in, get the woman, and get out. In. Out. And Will would be beside him, so there could be no way to be snared by temptation. The man had dragged him from more unsavory places than this one appeared to be.

"I don't think this is a sound move." Will tugged Oliver's jacket, a discreet pull on the expensive fabric. It was fast and unobtrusive but it got the message across.

Had the situation not been so threatening, he would never have placed a hand on Oliver in public.

"I agree. But there is nothing else to do, man." Oliver avoided an oncoming curricle with a couple of extra-long steps. Wincing as he came down hard on his left foot, he growled, "Botheration! She had to go in there? Damn it, why couldn't she have visited a dressmaker? A milliner? Anywhere but an establishment like this. Why? Why would she come here, of all places?"

He reached a hand out, lifted the heavy brass knocker, and struck it against the door three times.

"Why? Because parlor maids do not buy dresses

and hats on Bond Street. They sew their own, from lengths of fabric bought below stairs and shared amongst the help."

Oliver knew it must be true, although he had never before given any thought to his staff's apparel. Uniforms were a detail he did not trouble himself over. That was his mother's domain, not his.

Men provided the means to run a household. Women did the actual running.

Footsteps, heavy and hard, rapped against what he presumed to be a wooden floor. They grew louder.

Will spoke near his ear. "I really don't think we should go inside this den of iniquity. Why, if Vivian ever finds out I so much as stepped one foot over the threshold..."

Vivian, Oliver's distant relation, had wed Will six months earlier at Willowbrook Manor. They had met in the manor, fallen in love there, and made their vows in the rose garden. Now, they lived in a small cottage on the property.

"Why worry about Vivian? What are you—a man or a mouse?"

The door swung open to reveal a doorman who was so wide and tall it was impossible to see past his dark blue uniform. The sound of women's laughter, mixed with deeper, masculine voices, met their ears. A sweet scent, opium if Oliver guessed correctly, wafted out to greet them.

"Neither," Will answered, his voice low. "I'm married, and that trumps man or mouse in any situation. Someday, you'll understand that." He paused, then added, "That is, if we make it out of this whorehouse alive."

Chapter 2

"May I help you, gentlemen?" The blue wall looked like any ordinary butler although rather much bigger than was the norm. Facial features carefully arranged to give no hint to what was, even now, taking place beyond his broad back. He gave both Oliver and Will a brief inspection, gazing down to the tips of their shoes before looking askance once again at Will. "Sir?"

That he directed the conversation toward his help rather than to the Lord himself almost made Oliver grin. He sent a smallish nudge from his elbow to Will's, just the barest of touches to send the message to keep this charade going.

"Of course you may help us, my fine man." That his assistant could assume the upper class role so seamlessly, his tone a near-perfect imitation of his own, further amused Oliver. "We require admittance to your, ahem, establishment."

Again the man looked them over.

Finally, "Is Lady Panda expecting you?"

Lady Panda, indeed!

Will nearly choked but he managed a retort. "Why, of course we are expected. You do not think a peer would simply intrude on someone as renowned and respected as Lady Panda, do you? My word—how preposterous."

The man stepped back, unnerved by the bluster.

While he had been speaking, Will waved his walking stick through the air. At one point, Oliver had to duck to avoid being struck by the business end of the thing.

With a *hmmph!* he led the way, leaving Oliver to follow. Two steps behind his friend, he saw how the other's life must be. Not called upon to make a decision or be consulted about anything much. No voice in whether to stay or go, do or not do. Never a leader, always to tag behind. And while Will was not an unfortunate-looking sort, as fellows went, he was forced to admit the view was not altogether wonderful.

Watching another man's shoulders and backside as they brushed past the burly fellow was not the highlight of his day. But, they were in. And, no one could suspect that Lord Gregory of Willowbrook Manor and London was inside such a seedy residence.

Pocket doors of deep, mahogany wood led off a long, wide center corridor but they were all pulled closed. Low, laughing murmuring voices penetrated the dark wood but there was no way to ascertain to whom those hushed tones belonged.

The air was nearly lavender with smoke, a cloying scent borne on an air current that pulled it past his face in a steady stream. He wondered about the source of the air current, at the same time attempting not to breathe too deeply.

There was only one open door, and it was at the far end of the hallway. Will walked to it with such a fast pace that he was grateful his long legs were able to keep up, despite the aching ankle. A man of lesser stature may have had to scamper behind to maintain the position.

The room they entered was shadowy. Windows

obscured by tightly-drawn heavy brocade draperies kept the sun's position a mystery. Candlelight puddled on tabletops and in front of large, gilt-edged mirrors.

The only occupant who looked up when they entered the room was a young maid. Petite and despite her hair being neatly tucked into her white lace headwear, wisps of gold escaped to curl about her small ears. She looked like a ray of sunshine.

Entirely too young to be in a place reeking of smoke. She carried a silver tray topped with tumblers of amber liquid, which she immediately brought to them with a curtsey so practiced none of the glassware moved a bit.

"Lady Panda bids you welcome." Her voice was small, to match her size. "Please, help yourself to some refreshment."

Oliver did not respond, putting himself squarely in the role of unassuming manservant. Neither seen nor heard, that was the way of life his subterfuge cast him in. It was good, because the whiff of alcohol mixed with something even more intoxicating than the spirits wafted from the tumblers when she'd dipped.

The temptation to sample the beverage was non-existent. Only a stupid man falls in the same hole more than once. He hadn't nearly lost his life and battled desperately to scrabble out of the addiction trap to tumble into it a second time.

Never again, he had sworn. And, that was an oath he planned to keep.

Will, however, was denied the opportunity to wave the tray off. Not that he didn't try, regardless.

"Ahem…ah, no, thank you. I do not feel especially thirsty at this moment." He hadn't relinquished his walking stick to the man at the door, so he gave the floor a solid poke with it to punctuate his refusal.

"But, your Lordship, Lady Panda insists her guests be comfortable. Please, accept her hospitality." She gazed from one man to the other, and Oliver saw in her eyes what her lips would not divulge. She was instructed—no, obligated—to see the guests had a tumbler in hand shortly after their arrival. Depending on how stern the chain of command was in the household, the girl would most likely be punished if she did not properly carry out her duty. Perhaps a dressing down. Perhaps something more severe.

Oliver's mother ran Willowbrook with a firm hand but had never allowed any of their servants to be misused or inappropriately punished. Once or twice in his lifetime, there had been instant dismissals from service, but that had been the worst of it. And that had been for substantial infractions Mother deemed could not be corrected with a stern reprimand.

Fear showed plainly in the cornflower-blue eyes that glanced his way.

"I am sure Lady Panda means well, but I am not thirsty at this mom—"

Oliver cleared his throat. Loudly.

Will knew him well enough to pause.

They stood silent for a few moments.

He repeated the throat clearing. This time he gave Will a gentle bump on the back.

"Excuse me, your Lordship. I did not mean to bump."

Will turned to him. A smirk, and a glimmer in his eyes, gave his face a rakish appearance. "Your ankle, Mr. Greendick? It pains you, doesn't it?" He raised a pointed eyebrow, daring Oliver to take umbrage, before he turned a smile upon the young woman.

The maid swallowed a giggle but not so quickly that they did not hear the noise.

He nearly choked on the laughter that threatened to overtake him. Perhaps it was the smoke in the air that let his guard down a tad; he'd been trying not to inhale too deeply but one had to breathe.

He cleared his throat again, a swift glance at the maid confirming his suspicion that she was doing her best not to giggle. Who knew how long the young thing stood in this room, inhaling the strong, mind-altering smoke? It was a miracle she could keep to her feet the way she did.

Well, Will wasn't dealing with a schoolboy.

"I hate to say so, but it does indeed, Lord Gasball."

His assistant whirled around, his brows disappearing beneath his hairline. His eyes were huge circles on his usually placid face. Oliver met his gaze with a bland expression.

"Well, then we shall be swift, Greendick."

"I would appreciate that, Your Lordship." He waited a beat, then nodded toward the maid. She had covered her mouth with her free hand, her eyes brimming with unshed tears of mirth. "Perhaps the young woman is correct. It seems the thing to at least taste the libation. It does look thirst-quenching."

He shot a glance from the tumblers to the girl's eyes. She met his, but only for a second. It was enough to see she was overwhelmed by the effect of the smoky room. She was a small figure, but even a larger person would eventually succumb to the drug. They needed to leave as quickly as possible.

"As you say, Greendick."

Will chose the tumbler nearest the edge of the tray. He raised it to his face, put it beneath his nose, and inhaled. He did not touch it to his lips. Instead, he lowered the glass and leaned close to the maid.

"A rather indelicate question, I fear." He hesitated, looking down at his feet in what could only be called the greatest show of acting since the prior evening's theater production. "Ahem...I find I am in need of...that is to say, I would be in a better position to drink this rather appealing potion if I were to first...well, I'm sure you understand..."

Oliver could not help himself. He leaned close to the girl, winked, and announced, "Lord Gasbag does not have the greatest capacity for holding his water, I'm afraid. If we don't get him to the proper spot soon, I fear for Lady Panda's beautiful Persian carpet."

The girl motioned to the far end of the room.

"Through that door, gentlemen. Two doors down, on the right."

"Thank you." Oliver gave her a very small bow. "Your lordship, this way. Time to allow your little friend the chance to let the water fall."

As they threaded their way through the room, he noted that several gentlemen seated on the low settees scattered around the room held young, buxom women in their laps. Many smoked, both from conventional pipes as well as water-glass hookah pipes. It was no wonder the air was so thick.

The necessary room was, thankfully, unoccupied. They squeezed in the space, which was as gilded and ornate as the other room had been. Apparently Lady Panda believed her guests should be not only inebriated and in a smoky stupor but also pampered as they attended to the less elegant business.

Neither needed the room for its intended purpose, of course. There was so little room that they stood nearly nose to nose.

"Lord Gasbag? Did you truly just call me that?" Will grinned, not at all affronted by the title bestowed upon him. "I'm quite sure I don't mind that nearly as much as your implication regarding the size of my so-called 'little friend'—goodness, whatever were you thinking?"

"I was thinking that you called my friend green. Did you see the maid when you said that? I thought she was going to die trying to hold the laughter inside."

"Poor thing is probably discombobulated from being in that room." Will shook his head. "I know my mind is not nearly as clear as it ordinarily is, and I do not have to stand there hour after hour."

"I could not do it." He wished for a glass of water to wash the taste of inhaled smoke from his throat, but the only libation available to them was the glass the other still held. "You should dump that out. God only knows what it contains."

A collision with Oliver's elbow when he turned to put the tumbler on a wall ledge splashed onto Will's pants in a rather embarrassing spot. They both looked down at his crotch for a moment, too stunned to move.

Oliver chuckled. "Well should anyone see us in the hallway they will think you were too foxed to get yourself properly liberated."

"It is good that you are so amused. I certainly hope it dries without leaving a mark, or my wife will wonder what I've been up to."

"We could always use some of the water from that jug to, ah, wash the area." He pointed to the wide ledge running waist high around the room. Two china jugs held water for cleaning purposes. Not potable for drinking, since it was more than likely that the water had been drawn from the rain barrels, but it would work fine in this situation.

"It would make the spot considerably bigger. I will pass, and hope Vivian does not take notice."

"Just as well. We need to find that maid and get out of here." Oliver peeked his head out of the doorway. The corridor was empty. They exited and took it at a near run down the hallway away from the public room.

The house was not grand. It was not large, either. Finding the service areas was so much more straightforward than it would have been had they been at the Gregory estate.

They skidded to a stop in a kitchen that was tiny by comparison to the one at Willowbrook. Polished wide-plank floors and scrubbed preparation tables were wholly occupied. Staff moved about like a legion of worker bees, sidestepping and reaching as if it were a dance they performed to music only they could hear. The action stopped when they made their entrance.

All heads turned and everyone stared. Even the child polishing boots near the doorway paused, boot brush mid-swipe.

Oliver looked from person to person. None was the one they searched for. Botheration! So many maids, and none the one they wanted? Where was the justice in that?

It was only a matter of time before someone realized Lord Gasbag and his manservant had disappeared, so he smiled and asked, "Has anyone seen a maid?"

They all looked at each other as if the pair were Bedlam escapees. Shrugged.

A man spoke up. "Your Lordship, we all see several maids. Don't you, sir?"

"Of course he does." Will rolled his eyes and gave them a conspiratorial wink. "His Lordship has, um, well, he's imbibed a good amount of Lady Panda's potent potable. So, you see…"

He spread his arms wide, a gesture of helplessness but as he did, his coat parted and the wet splotch on his crotch came into view. All gazes dropped. The little shoeshine boy laughed and pointed with the shoe on his hand.

Will turned red-cheeked but went on like one of the King's guards. "We seek a young woman who came in off the street a short while ago. A scant half-hour ago, perhaps. She has a position with a dear friend of ours, and we simply wish to ask a favor of her." When the manservant frowned, he added, "A perfectly respectable favor, I assure you. We are…ah, we are planning a surprise for her employer and wish to know some of her favorite foods so our kitchen may prepare the best birthday feast imaginable. Makes life easier, doesn't it, when one knows what another likes best?"

The feebleness of explanation left the servants silent for several long minutes. Then, the child pointed to a doorway.

"She went in there, she did. Came to see Old Dorinda, just like the others."

"Hush." The cook flapped her white apron at the boy, but he batted it with the shoe.

"Well she did. Just like the rest of 'em, coming for the potion."

"Quiet, child," the manservant said but before the words left his mouth they were at the plain wooden door.

Oliver did not knock. He pressed the latch, pushed the door open, and stepped inside.

An old woman looked up from a scarred pine worktable. She crushed something in a rough wooden pestle with a mortar held by a gnarled fist. She looked to be a hundred, although that was hardly possible.

Her voice was soft and gentle, the sound of a stream over worn rocks. Nothing prepared Oliver for the melodious words or the lack of outrage over being burst in upon.

"Well, well. What have we here? Two fine gentlemen coming to see Old Dorinda?"

Will closed the door behind them when it seemed the manservant would follow. He placed his back against the door.

Crossing the room, Oliver searched for something to say. There was no one in sight save the potionist. A door leading to what he presumed to be a back alleyway was the only egress from the space aside from through the kitchen door they'd just used. And since the child indicated the maid went in but said nothing of her going back out, he deduced she had exited through the alleyway door.

She crushed some dried green leaves. Others, mostly the same variety but a few of different shape, as well as a pile of desiccated red berries were heaped beside her mortar. Oliver did not recognize any of them but he was totally unskilled in the art of potion-making.

He had witnessed the effects of some rather harsh concoctions during his dark time, but he had never cared to sample any. It was one of the only substances he declined, although he had no idea why he had done so. Now he wished he had even a rudimentary knowledge. He had no idea what to ask the old woman, aside from the obvious.

"Excuse us for barging in the way we have, but time is of the essence." When she did not respond, he went on. "We are in search of a young woman. She came in off the street, and we are fairly certain she came to see you."

"You are not planning a party, are you?"

How did she decipher their faradiddle? They weren't speaking loudly in the next room, and the walls were brick—and probably ten inches thick. It was improbable she overheard yet she knew their fib. How?

No time to ponder. Oliver shook his head. "No. We are not arranging a party. We just need to ask the woman a few questions."

"Are either of you involved with this young lady?" She paused, gave her attention to the mixture. The rasp of wood on wood as she ground leaves was a soothing, rhythmic sound. She did not look up when she spoke. "If you are part of the situation…well, I have the means to render you unable to bring this occasion upon yourself—and the poor woman you've assaulted—again."

"Now wait a minute! I did not—"

She cut him off, airily waving the pestle through the air as she added berries to the mixture.

"I did not say I would render you incapable of performing, your lordship. Rather, it would be impossible to get a woman in a certain predicament as long as you ingested my potion." She put the instrument down, wiped her hands down the front of her serviceable brown work dress and met his gaze. Oliver saw the wisdom of many years in those eyes.

Once, while on safari on the African continent, he met a wizened medicine man whose knowledge danced behind ageless eyes. This was the second time he'd seen the world behind a gaze. If he were the quickly frightened type, he would have backed away but he wasn't so he stood his ground.

It crossed his mind the woman might be toying with him. To assume she told the truth would be foolish.

"Oh, yes." A sage nod. "You are not the man responsible. Well, no matter. I can offer the same service to you. Your servant as well. He seems predisposed to troubled emissions."

Oliver grinned, remembering the wet patch on the other's trousers. He couldn't help himself. He didn't need to turn to know Will was nearly beside himself with indignation and embarrassment.

"Your offer is generous, but neither of us has need for that service." He glanced at the door. "She went that way, didn't she? And you are chatting us up so she has adequate time to disappear into the crowd on the street, aren't you?"

Old Dorinda shot him a contented smile. "I had you picked for a keen wit. You have caught my motivation. By now, the woman you seek is lost to the morning foot traffic. You, sirs, have wasted your time on a fool's errand." She rapped the pestle on the tabletop. "And that is the job of fools, isn't it?"

Chapter 3

Willowbrook Manor was situated far enough from Town that it felt like the country, yet was close enough that social events, shopping expeditions and ordinary business ventures were a short ride. Oliver's father, the aged and somewhat infirm Lord Gregory, kept a house in the city regardless. It proved convenient when affairs ran late or the weather was especially troublesome.

Will and Oliver had spent the night in the London house. After a couple of hours watching Lady Panda's entrance from a concealed spot a few doors down Bond Street, they had been tired and hungry, but no closer to speaking with the maid. A quick dinner at a loud pub, where they were prepared to continue the charade of Greendick and Gasbag had anyone inquired. They were both somewhat disappointed that no one did ask, so they were reduced to referring to each other with the mildly inappropriate monikers at every opportune moment.

Oliver drove like he did everything else, with purpose and complete capability. He handled the horses without effort, and the animals recognized his touch as that of a true horseman so they responded in kind. The ride, taken on such a sunny morning, was a pleasant one.

"I do wish we had located that young woman last night." Will removed his hat and turned his face to the sky. He closed his eyes. "It would have saved us a lot of trouble if she had returned."

"How so?"

He rotated his face slightly and opened only the left eye. "We both know that you are like a dog after a bone and will not give up. You mean to find out what that woman is about. And, I know I am going to be dragged along on the adventure."

Oliver snorted. Had their lots in life been different, he and William Fulbright would be best friends. Better yet, that they might have been brothers. But Will was not a peer, so the best they could achieve was close-as-brothers when alone, and lord with manservant in public.

When he had been overcome with his addictive tendencies and nearly lost his life to drug usage, Will had been the one to pull him from the clutches of his deviant behavior. He had taken him back to Willowbrook when he had been so afflicted he was reduced to screaming like a madman and two steps from being admitted into an asylum. His life had been saved by the man beside him. And that was a debt that could never be repaid—peerage, social standing and propriety be damned.

"Will, you know me well. I do intend to find that maid and get the truth from her." He gave the reins a quick twitch. The horses responded instantly, quickening their pace.

"And I am your cohort."

"Are you complaining?"

Will's eyes remained closed, his head tilted to the sun. "Certainly not."

"I am sure I can find another manservant, if you

are." That his companion looked as relaxed as a young boy on holiday crossed his mind.

"Bite your tongue. Oliver, you know I am on you like sticking glue on dentures."

He chuckled. They were at the edge of the property, so he turned the horses onto the wide, tree-lined lane. Will sat up straight and put his hat back in place. It would not do to have a stray grounds man see the future of the estate driving his carelessly-clad assistant about.

Propriety, the bane of the upper class, dictated they appear distant in front of prying eyes. But the family and their closest friends knew the truth: Oliver couldn't love Will more if he had been born his blood brother.

"Are you saying I am tooth powder?"

Will shook his head, smiling as he elbowed him. "Quite the contrary. I am the tooth powder. You, Mister Greendick, are the dentures!"

He had learned the hard way not to take any day for granted, so now he threw his head back and let his amusement surface. They pulled up to the front of the manor that way, he laughing like a man who had just heard the merriest joke in the pub and Will concealing his own smile behind a hand.

He tossed the reins to the boy who waited to claim them. They climbed down and went inside. Instantly the sound of female voices met their ears.

Oliver turned to Will. "It seems your bride is here. I hear that lovely tinkling laugh she possesses. You are a fortunate man to have made such a brilliant match."

The other did not try to hide his love. He nodded, his smile bigger than ever. "Indeed I am."

****

A fire roared cheerily in the grate and brought the temperature of the room so high the windows were opened to admit a breeze. Still, the air did not blow away Amy's feeling that the world was about to fall in on her. Living with the trepidation that nothing was as it should be was taking its toll. Too, hiding the truth from those she loved most dearly was a burden almost too heavy to carry.

Her sister, Miranda, sat closest to the door so when the men entered, she saw them first. And since Oliver led the way into the room, she acted in typical Miranda fashion. How one could fall so obviously at a man's feet when the man in question had made it demonstrably clear her affections were not reciprocated was beyond comprehension.

Still, Miranda tittered.

"Ladies, good morning to one and all." Oliver bent at the waist, extended a leg and acted as if they were at Almack's rather than the front sitting room. He nodded to each of them in turn.

"Lucie, looking lovely this morning. Is my brother-in-law expected home today?"

Lucie placed her embroidery on her lap. "Nick should be back sometime this afternoon. I cannot wait; Mother is hovering over me in uncharacteristic fervor. It makes me quite cross, all this fluttering and flapping."

The ever-solicitous older sibling, Oliver brought his brows together. "Whatever has her going on about? You look perfectly healthy to me, and you are certainly accustomed to your husband's comings and goings. He does have vast holdings to attend, after all."

"You and I know that, but apparently Mother does

not. It is, I am sure, just that she is habitual about hovering over someone. With Father feeling better, she has turned her attention onto me. Do a sister a favor, won't you? Capture some of her attention for yourself. I am nearly done in assuring her I am fine. Well fed. Happy. I beg you, Oliver, let her dote on you for a bit. She is killing me with this kindness."

"I will do what I can." He turned his gaze on Vivian, their distant cousin who had married his best friend. Will stood behind his bride's chair. She had dropped her sewing onto her lap and had a hand on her husband's where it lay on her shoulder.

They looked happier than any two people had a right to look. Vivian shone, pure radiance coming from her in waves. Amy hated herself, but she was jealous.

"How are you, cousin? Keeping well, I hope?"

Vivian blushed, ever-so-slightly. She and Will had let it be known there would be an addition to their family by the New Year. The only indication she was with child was the glow in her eyes when she looked at her adoring husband.

Amy's own stomach flip-flopped dangerously. The grippe she had been battling for the past two weeks threatened to return so she swallowed hard and concentrated on not being sick.

"I am, thank you. It is such a beautiful day…how could anyone be anything other than hale and hearty?" When Oliver made a deliberate show of leaning forward to examine the scrap of fabric in her lap, Vivian giggled. Holding the tiny garment up for inspection, she sighed. "I suppose it is no secret that I am hoping for a boy. Will urges me to make the newborn clothing either green or yellow, or even white, but I favor blue. It is to be a boy; I am certain of it so why waste time with neutral fabric?"

Ever the jolly fellow, Oliver raised one eyebrow so high on his forehead it nearly disappeared beneath a curl that had fallen forward. "What? No pink?"

She feigned a shudder. "No pink. Aren't there enough females in this family already? Besides, Liam is hoping for a nephew."

Her mother and younger brother lived nearby, in a cottage large enough to afford room for the dressmaking business she conducted. That turn of events was a result of Vivian's marriage. Before coming to Willowbrook Manor, she and her family lived in Stropshire in a very small, drafty flat.

"*Hmmph.*" Oliver grinned at Will. "And what if Uncle Oliver wants a niece? What then?"

"He shall have to wait, just like the rest of us, to see what comes of this. Boy or girl, it matters not to me." Will rubbed a tender hand across the back of his wife's neck. "I just want a healthy babe, and a healthy mother. Although, I do admit, I would not mind rocking a daughter in my arms…"

"Hush." His wife gave a playful slap at the hand. "I'm sewing blue swaddling, so the little one will have to be a boy."

"Who can argue with logic like that?" Oliver shrugged, then turned his attention on her and her sister. His gaze swept from one to the other, and when he looked at Miranda she once again tittered. "Miss Spencer. And, Miss Spencer. Sisters of my heart, it is nice to see you here."

"Why so formal?" Miranda, dressed in her signature blue, had twin blooms of pink on her cheeks that grew deeper when she spoke.

Amy never wanted to be that taken with a man that she could not control her complexion. It was a shame, that a bluestocking of her sister's magnitude could be reduced to ninny-hood by a man's presence.

It made her sick. And, the grippe sent a fresh wave of nausea rolling over her. Perspiration broke out on her forehead and upper lip. She dabbed her face with the edge of a spare length of linen. The thread for the blanket she worked fell on the floor beside her chair but to bend over and pick it up was risky given the state of her stomach so she did not move.

Oliver, ever the gentleman, tucked his hands into his jacket pockets and smiled.

"Why, with all this important discussion of the family growing and all, it hardly seems the time for informality. But, it is a pleasant surprise, indeed, to find you looking so lovely this morning. And, it seems you are also busy preparing for the newcomer."

"Yes, we are all helping to build a tiny wardrobe." Miranda held up a little nightgown for him to admire. It was mint green with miniscule flowers embroidered at the neckline and along the hem. "I chose the green…just in case." She blushed even more furiously, as if the comment in reference to childbirth was much too intimate.

The desire to slap her sister was instant. Falling in love with a man who didn't feel the same way was one of the most idiotic things a woman could do. God help her, she knew that better than anyone in the room—even dopey-faced Miranda.

Oliver turned his attention her way just as her stomach gave a precarious lurch.

"And you, Amy…what beautiful bit of baby finery are you working on over there?"

She stood, covering her mouth with the tiny garment and ran for an open window. How she managed to reach it in time was beyond her but she leaned over the wide window sill and lost the contents of her stomach to the flower bed below.

It was not one of her finest moments. And, it did little to enhance the beauty of the baby gown she'd been working.

Chapter 4

When Amy opened her eyes, sunlight streamed low through the window in the large, airy front bedroom. It had been Lucie's room all the years she lived at the manor. Then, Vivian stayed in the massive bed when she came for the Season. Now, she and Miranda occupied the room when they visited.

She looked around. There was no sign of Miranda. Or her things.

Laying back against the wall of soft feather pillows, she reasoned her sister had moved to one of the other guest rooms. Either to keep herself from catching what ailed her or to give some peace to the sickroom, Amy could not guess. It was near impossible to understand the workings of her sister's mind.

Besides, she had more pressing issues to ponder.

One in particular. One who had disappeared almost as mysteriously as he had appeared at her coming-out party. The guest list had been so long, an unending column, with most of the invited peers people she would never meet again or friends of her parents. Only one name mattered to her now. Until she had been formally presented to Lyle Roarke, the son of a lesser earl, she had no idea he even existed, but his was the name from the auspicious event that would not be forgotten.

The moment she saw him she became enamored.

Their acquaintance had turned romantic. Rides in the country. Musicales in the moonlight. Whist games. Cotillions. All under the watchful eye of Society, of course. Every now and then, she could coax her sister into covering for her while she and Lyle stole a moment in the shadows. But aside from a few heated interludes—during which her clothing was never removed—theirs had been a romance above reproach. Or, mostly above reproach.

Until recently. And, the event that changed the course of her life.

Then, Lyle's disappearance.

Finally, her grippe. A clear case of nerves, worrying if she'd be publicly ruined.

A quiet knock. Before she could call out, the door opened and Lucie's head appeared. A smile as she entered carrying a tray and kicking the door closed behind her.

Marriage agreed with her dear friend. She looked older and wiser, and although the duke traveled a great deal, she still seemed content.

Lucie placed the tray on the bedside table.

"How are you feeling? Any better?"

Pushing herself to a sitting position, Amy settled in against the pillows while Lucie prepared two cups of tea. She accepted hers gratefully, taking a small sip to gauge the condition of her stomach. It seemed fine, so she took a larger sip of the sweetened, hot Earl Grey.

"Thank you. I am, actually." She held the cup and saucer while her visitor perched on the edge of the bed. Then she placed the saucer on the bedclothes, on her lap. The china cup had a dainty handle, but she kept a two-finger hold on it.

"I am glad to hear that. You have had us all worried."

"It is just a case of the grippe. Nothing to be concerned about." She took another sip, hoping the conversation was over.

It wasn't.

"Be that as it may, I have sent for Doctor Fairweather. He should examine you, just to be sure nothing serious is going on."

Ice ran in Amy's veins.

"Absolutely not—I will not be examined. I tell you, I am fine. Just a case of the grippe. My tummy took a bad turn, is all. It happens to everyone. I will not consent to mollycoddling or interference from a dodgy old doctor."

"How can you say such things? And how on earth can you call Doctor Fairweather dodgy? Goodness gracious, but that wonderful man has taken excellent care of all of us—you, Miranda, me, Oliver—since we were in swaddling clothes. It is most uncharitable of you to refuse to see the man. Why, he is coming to be of service, and on your account."

She swallowed a lump in her throat. Her emotions rode high lately, and this sudden burst of near-crying hit out of the blue.

"I am sorry. You are right, but I still won't see him. I am fine, Lucie. I do not want to be examined."

"You should be, though."

"I refuse." There was little she could control in her life, but this something she would not allow.

Lucie kept silent, and drank some of her tea. She motioned toward a plate of scones on the tray, but Amy could not even look at them. She shook her head.

Taking a scone and carefully balancing it on her saucer beside her cup took some concentration, but once it was accomplished, Lucie cleared her throat.

"You have not been yourself lately, Amy. I fear some of the blame for your, ah, distance is mine. I know I have not been as faithful in my friendship as I should be now that I am a married woman." She paused, took a thoughtful bite and chewed. Then, she swallowed and met her gaze. Unshed tears made her eyes shine when she said, "I am new to being a wife, even though Nick and I have been married over a year now. There is much to learn, many things to overcome—even in a happy marriage, there are matters to deal with. They have, I fear, kept me busy to the point of neglecting you and Miranda. Truly, I am so very sorry."

A huge lump swelled in Amy's throat. She could barely breathe, it grew so large.

Shaking her head, she rushed to reassure her dearest friend.

"No, it is not your fault. Nothing is your fault. And you are not like us anymore—"

"Oh, how could you say such a thing?" The tears fell onto her closest friend's cheeks now.

She sat forward and pulled Lucie into an embrace. Tea and the scone went flying, but the two put their arms about each other. Lucie put her face down and sobbed.

She had no idea why the other cried, but Amy knew it was more than a lapse in friendship. They had been close as sisters their entire lives, all three of them, so tears and hurt feelings were nothing new. This, however, was more serious in nature. The tears were an adult's heartache, not a skinned knee or misplaced locket.

Eventually the torrent subsided. Still, she held her tightly, rubbing her hand along Lucie's back and waiting until the sniffling was nearly over. Then she sat back, handed over the clean lace hanky she kept inside her sleeve and watched the other blow her nose. Twice.

"Feel better now?" She suddenly felt older and wiser, although they were both four-and-twenty.

A sniff. Then, a slow nod. "I do."

"Do you feel like talking about it? I am, as you well know, a very good listener."

Lucie shook her head.

"Is it because I am not Miranda?"

That garnered a puzzled expression. When the other opened her mouth, she held up a hand to stem the protest.

"It is not as if I don't know what you two say about me when I am out of earshot. Really, I know you are closer to my sister than me. She is more serious, a true bluestocking and someone who would never, ever get herself into any manner of bumble broth." Amy ran a hand over the bed covering where it had been splashed with tea. The spot was drying but would leave a mark against the white fabric. "While I, as you are both so fond of telling me, am far too wild by far to be taken as anything more than a lark."

Lucie inhaled sharply. Being called out on the truth of things had to put her a step back, but the pair had spoken thusly for years. What, had she no feelings? Had she no right to protest the labels the two more serious of the trio heaped upon her? Had she no right to speak the truth—especially when all she wanted was to be of some help?

To someone. For something. Sometime.

Botheration! Her life had turned so completely inside out that her best friend wouldn't even confide in her.

"Amy…"

"Don't try to deny it." She met Lucie's gaze. To her credit, her friend's eyes were not only puffy from crying but chagrined as the truth of their association came out between them. "I have known all along, have felt the odd duck out for some time now. It is no one's fault."

"I don't know what to say. I have completely let you down, haven't I?"

She took a deep breath. Her sides hurt from retching, and she was swept over by a wave of supreme exhaustion. The effort of speaking seemed too much, so she shook her head and snuggled down into the pillows and blankets.

"We have let each other down, I think." A yawn, so big it hurt her sides when she stretched to cover her mouth. "Now, if you will please leave me to my grippe. I am very, very tired."

It was a ghastly impolite thing to do, but she turned on her side, facing away from her visitor. She closed her eyes and, not caring a whit what Lucie thought, went to sleep.

Chapter 5

Oliver reached the fencing area long before his friend. He planned it that way. One of his favorite times of the day was early morning, when darkness gave in to light. Sunrise above the east meadow was spectacular, the way it had been since he was a boy and had crept from his bed—much to Nanny Greta's annoyance—and run to his perch in the limb of the massive oak beneath which he now sat.

The tea had long ago cooled down, but he did not mind. As he sipped, he thought about the events unfolding at the estate. Since his recovery from addiction he had claimed the responsibility for almost every aspect of operations, save the household details. Those were still, thankfully, handled by his mother.

His parents were better than they had been in some time. If his father was well enough to be about, riding, visiting with his cronies and buying cigars in Town, his heart must be sturdier than before and recovering. And, his mother's meddling in Lucie's life was a sign that she wasn't so preoccupied with Father's health that she didn't have a moment to spare for anything—or anyone—else. Good for Mother, hard on his sister.

And Lucie…since she and Nick, a well-known duke, were wed, her life had changed drastically. Or, it should have. While she wasn't supposed to be still living at Willowbrook, she spent many days and nights in the suite of rooms she and Nick had begun using as their own on their wedding night. The duke was a wealthy man, with many properties and people who depended on him. He wasn't one to let an assistant or solicitor do what he was able to do himself. Therefore, he was away from his new bride more than Oliver, in his humble, bachelor, opinion, thought prudent.

He didn't like the way Lucie's manner had grown so subdued. Her customarily bubbly personality was no more, and he didn't care for that one little bit. He wanted his sister back but had no idea how to bring that about.

"You look in a blue study." Will had approached on silent feet, but that was his norm so Oliver did not start when the man's polished brown boots appeared beside him. Will gazed down at him with a worried expression. "Is everything as it should be? Are you well?"

He crouched, bringing them at eye level with one another. Oliver waved off the probing examination.

"I am fine, don't worry so much. I've had nothing stouter than tea for well over a year, and I am not inclined to partake of anything stronger." He drained the dregs from his mug and set it at the base of the tree. "I am simply taking stock of the situation here at the estate. Quite a lot to order in one's mind."

The other man pulled fencing gloves onto his hands, pressing his fingers into the soft leather and fisting each hand to warm them.

"Yes, indeed. I am glad I don't have your responsibilities on my shoulders. It would prove too much for me to handle."

"Don't underestimate yourself. You would fare

well if the roles were reversed." He watched a fat red robin work to pull his breakfast from the grass. The worm, for his part, resisted, holding deeply onto the soil. "We are all dug in here, our lives intertwined with each other as well as the estate. I cannot let anyone down. I need to be certain everyone is cared for properly, and wants for nothing. That is how Father has always been, and it is how I shall be, as well."

"There is no one who is lacking here. You are entirely too serious sometimes. All is well—unless of course you remember poor Amy's tummy. I do hope she is improved this morning. Vivian did not want to discuss it, but she did allow that yesterday was not the first time she has been violently ill."

"Not good. It is interesting that no one else has fallen ill. We are, after all, a close group."

"Good point. Although I am glad my wife did not share the illness. We…ah…"

He grinned, and Will returned the smile. Their close bond included sharing secrets the way blood brothers might.

"You two had a nice night, then?"

A brisk nod, then he slapped his hands together. "We did at that."

"It's allowed…with the babe coming, and all?" The bachelor life did not include facts regarding women's health, so he deferred to his married, and much wiser in that respect, assistant.

"Doctor Fairweather told her it's perfectly fine to be…ah, well, in that situation, for a while longer yet. I was surprised, but she does not seem to mind and, well, I certainly won't put an end to that sort of thing prematurely."

"Women are really stronger than we give them credit for, aren't they?"

"Yes, I believe they are much stronger than we are, even. Certainly, our muscles are bigger and we are heavier, but when I think that my beautiful Vivian is going to bring forth a child from her own body—that slender, perfect body—it renders me speechless. If I were called upon to do such a thing, I do not believe I could do it. I do not have the fortitude for such a task."

The robin was still after the worm. Oliver watched, then shooed the bird away with a fast wave of his arm. He'd been tenacious, but the worm had also refused to give up, so it seemed fair the worm deserved to live another day.

"I am in complete awe of the female sex. If they left it to us, the human race would have surely come to a screeching halt with Adam and Eve." He pushed himself to his feet, brushed the seat of his trousers off and grabbed his fencing gloves. As he put them on, he grinned at Will. "Do you think you've energy enough to parry with me for a bit?"

"I always have enough energy for fencing. You know that." He picked up his foil, removed the protective leather sleeve covering the pointed tip and stabbed the air a few times.

Oliver walked toward the center of the clearing. The sun was fully up and the morning grew warm. Dew evaporated off the lush grass and birdsong surrounded them. It was a good start to the day, vigorous exercise in the freshest air this side of Town.

"Then I suggest you put your best foot forward." Oliver grinned as he lunged and struck his opponent on the shoulder. All in fun, a test shot, warming up exercise to start the competition. He stood down, waiting for Will to take his position and raise his foil. "Because I have the distinct advantage of having slept soundly, with no drain on my energy level. You, of course, cannot say quite the same, can you?"

"*Hmmph!*" Will struck, a solid movement which would draw blood had he not held back on his force. "It is obvious you do not know much about marital relations. If you did, you would realize that there are times a man is energized by his wife's ministrations. Unfortunately for you, this is one of those times." Two hours later, Will and Oliver made their way into the front sitting room. They were not so grimy that they would attract undue attention, although Will did have a small rip in the shoulder of his white shirt.

Lady Gregory looked up from her book when they entered. She was alone, which surprised her son. He expected all the women to be gathered, doing whatever women did on a beautiful afternoon.

"Mother." He crossed the room, bent down, and placed a kiss on her soft cheek. As always, she smelled of talc and rosewater. "I hope I am not intruding."

She waved him toward the seat nearest hers. Will left quietly, most likely going in search of Vivian. At the very least, to change his shirt.

Crossing one leg over another, he sat back. Despite the exercise he'd just given it, his left ankle was none the worse for the wear. It was mending, and he was grateful to heal so quickly. Infirmity robbed a man of precious time, forced one to sit rather than run, and he hated that idea.

He took a moment to assess his mother's mood. She appeared serene, but that was no guarantee she was of that mind. One could never tell the disposition of a woman upon casual observation. They were, in his opinion, too complex for most men to decipher.

She was alone. That meant one of two things: Either she wanted solitude or had been left behind. He could not tell which might be a better situation.

"You could never intrude, Oliver. I am glad to see you for I am, I admit, bored with my own company."

He looked around. The sitting room had not changed in decades. Chintz fabric. Cozy reading alcoves. Two fireplaces, one in a far corner to chase away winter drafts and the main hearth, where even now a small pile of oak logs burned.

"Where is everyone? It is almost unsettling to have it be so quiet in here."

"Yes, I agree. I am somewhat out of sorts over being the only one with nothing better to do than sit here with my nose in Miss Austen's book."

He glanced at the well-read volume. It had passed through every woman's hand at some point. Most, more than once.

"It is a good book, at least." He had not read it, but he'd heard it had some value.

"Oh, yes. It is entertaining. It will never become a classic, mind you. Too many silly turns of phrase and undue distresses, but it does pass the time."

Oliver hoped to find Bridget but could not simply turn and leave without chatting. When she offered him some tea, he shook his head.

"No, thank you. I fear I have much to do before dinnertime. But where is everyone? Father?"

"He is with Hugh, showing off his stables."

Hugh Upton, a lesser earl who was very fond of

horses, frequently spent time talking horseflesh with anyone who would listen. He and the duke had been friends since they were children.

"And the women? So many women, yet the place is empty…it does not make sense."

He placed a hand on his brow and pantomimed searching for the missing beneath the table beside him. When he came up empty, he shrugged. And, his mother laughed, the way he hoped she might.

"It does seem strange, doesn't it? Well, Vivian, Lucie, and Miranda are in Town. Lucie declared she needed a change of scenery and wouldn't allow refusal from the others. She is, I believe, pining for her husband."

As he suspected.

"Nick is not here much."

She shook her head. The carefully pinned up curls never moved, prodigiously secured by the lady's maid who had done the same to those locks for nearly as long as he was alive.

"No, he isn't. And that has your sister—and me, if I am to be blunt—less than pleased with the situation. Goodness, they are still newly married. He should pay more attention to his wife and less to his holdings."

It was bold, but he asked. "Are you certain he is attending to business and not a private matter?"

Lady Gregory was not stupid. She understood and shook her head almost before the words passed his lips.

"No, it is nothing untoward. Nick is far too upstanding to sink that low. No, I am certain he is just accustomed to being unattached and doing as he pleases. He has not yet realized that he needs to spend more time with her. Especially if…" She shrugged. Her figure, so delicate and elegantly clothed, belied the attitude that was more wistful than lady of the manor-ish.

"If what, Mother? They are happy, aren't they?"

"I have no doubt that when they are together, they are quite happy. It's just that your father and I would like grandbabies. And that requires both parties spend at least some time in the same location."

"Yes, I do see what you mean." He did not wish to interfere...but perhaps a friendly, brother-to-brother talk? Time to change the subject, he thought. No telling where this might lead. "You've accounted for everyone except Amy. Did she go to Town as well?"

A soft sigh, and a tiny head shake. Sadness and worry infused his mother's voice. "No, I am afraid she did not feel up to going."

He glanced at the window where Amy had unceremoniously leaned out yesterday. "Has the doctor been summoned?"

"More than once, but she refuses to see him. I have tried to reason with her, as have Lucie and Vivian, but she is adamant. Not even Miranda can influence her." A short pause, then she added, "I am concerned, Oliver. The Spencers trust us to treat their daughters as our own, and we always have. If our Lucie were this ill, I would not give her leave to refuse Doctor Fairweather. But..."

She clasped her hands in her lap, looking the picture of parental dejection.

Another talk to have, he thought as he reached out and patted his mother's hand. And soon.

Chapter 6

Lady Drabble's hair salon was by far the most prestigious in all of London. The eccentric woman was whispered to be a favorite of the Queen herself. Known for elaborate details, such as ostrich feathers, animal headdresses and cascades of jeweled curls, she was very difficult to see and refused more business than she accepted. She was smart enough, however, to never refuse Lady Lucie Grayson, the handsome Duke of Waterford's wife.

Lucie had sent her Abigail early to secure the time with the hairdresser. As she expected, she had not been turned away. And, she made it clear that, as was her custom, her female companions would require attention.

Lucie looked at herself in the wide glass window just beyond Lady Drabble's. It was just a surreptitious glance, because she knew all too well that there was no such thing as privacy, especially when out and about. The street had eyes, from the street sweeper who admired three elegantly-turned-out women to the maids scurrying past, errand lists clutched in work-worn hands. Everyone saw everything—and one must be conscious of being observed at every turn.

Still, she peeked. And liked what she saw.

If she were ever going to keep her husband at home, she must be as comely as possible. A new hair style would surprise Nick. Hopefully, it would entice him to stay in her bed and admire the artful locks long past the point he typically excused himself to begin his day.

He came home tonight. She had plans for them…

"You do look lovely, Lucie." Miranda touched her arm, the rustle of blue silk a soft sound as her gloves swept over Lucie's pelisse. "Nick will be enchanted when he sees those curls. Lady Drabble outdid herself today."

Vivian smiled from one to the other. She had asked for a more sedate hairstyle, claiming a married woman in her state neither needed nor wanted elaborately teased locks. The simple upsweep suited her delicate features. And the tiny violets tucked above her ear accented the violet eyes that were simply unforgettable.

"Thank you both. I am…well, I am hopeful that Nick will think me as lovely as you do."

Vivian raised an eyebrow. They were cousins, albeit removed cousins, so she had a familial link that excused an overstepped boundary.

"Are you and Nick having difficulties? I know it is a private matter, but after all we are relations, and I am a married woman, as well. Do you need advice? Not that I am so long married to have learned much of anything overly useful," she said with a little laugh.

She looked from friend to cousin. They were as sisters and could be trusted. It had been eating her from the inside out, this disagreeable business. Perhaps sharing the problem would give her an altogether new perspective.

They walked abreast, a slow stroll along the wide sidewalk. The park beckoned, so they turned onto the path and meandered through the greenery. Splendid to see the forest in the center of the city. And children playing by the pond brought all three to attention. They stopped, watching as a child dressed in full spring regalia, including high-top, side-button shoes, attempted to chase a ball across the grass. He had trouble moving, the shoes looking too tight and stiff to allow his small ankles to bend naturally.

"That is the thing," Lucie said quietly. She nodded to the child, who had just thrown his body atop the ball. Giggling, he tried to stand with it in his arms but toppled over onto his head. He laughed, tossing the ball high in the air. "Nick and I have been…well, we are hoping for…"

"You want a baby," Miranda said. Always straight to the point, never inclined to stay quiet—unless Oliver was within earshot. Then, she was very often unfortunately tongue-tied. It came from having a crush on him since they were children. Some things a woman outgrew; others did not pass into history as swiftly. Oliver had made it very clear he had no romantic inclination toward Miranda but that did not keep the woman's heart from working harder when the object of its affection was anywhere nearby.

Lucie smiled. She looked from Miranda to Vivian, then back to the little boy. His nanny had rescued him, putting him on his feet, and handing the ball into his outstretched arms. He toddled across the grass with it clutched to his chest. It was evident that it would not be long before the ball got away from him once again.

"Yes. We both want a child. Actually, we want more than one. But…"

"No success yet." Miranda stated the obvious.

"None," Lucie admitted. She sighed, hugging her arms around her midsection. "I keep thinking that if I can manage to keep him home longer, we shall have a chance. It is not easy when the husband is busy looking after other matters."

"Give it time," Vivian advised. "Relax. Enjoy your husband. It will happen in its own good time." She patted her stomach. She hadn't yet begun to bloom, which was good. When she did, she would not be as comfortable bouncing to the city in a carriage or being seen about Town. The confinement would begin soon, but for now her figure did not give her secret away.

"I need to keep that husband home long enough to…well, you know."

Miranda colored ever-so slightly. Then, she sighed. "I cannot wait until I have such problems. Imagine, a beautiful home. A handsome husband—and a duke, no less. And evenings spent in front of a roaring fire, rolling about on a fur rug in each other's arms."

Vivian and Lucie exchanged startled glances.

Lucie poked her dear friend in the shoulder. "Goodness, whatever have you been reading? A fine imagination you have, you goose." She leaned closer to Vivian and gave the other a poke with her elbow. "She does not yet realize that the floor is drafty, no rug is thick enough to keep an unforgiving floor from being hard, and it is not at all romantic when your husband burns his bottom on a flying ember, does she?"

Chapter 7

"I am glad you agreed to have dinner in private, in our rooms."

Lucie gazed at Nick across the remnants of the roast beef, mashed parsnips and boiled carrot dinner they had just finished. He chewed the last of his meat, wiped his mouth and sighed.

"Why, I don't believe there is anywhere else I would rather be, my dear. In private, in our own wing of this manse, all alone to amuse ourselves as we see fit…"

There was, as was always the case, much more food served than they could possibly eat but that's what the silver domes left by the staff were for. She covered the dishes, dropped her napkin onto her plate, and turned her attention on her husband. Tomorrow morning, the maids would clear the mess away. They had been instructed not to disturb the duke and duchess tonight, and for very good reason.

Lucie planned a seduction like no other. Nick might be tired from his long travels, but she intended to make him forget the journey and concentrate on his arrival. In their bed. And if they were fortunate, they might precipitate an arrival of their own…say, in nine months' time.

She pushed her chair back and waved him down when he would have stood. "I am fine, stay seated. I like the way you think, my love." The distance from her end of their small dining table to his was not long. She stopped behind his chair, put her arms around his shoulders, and lay her head against the mop of black curls she loved so much. "I don't want to seem forward, but I do have some things in mind that I think you may find very amusing."

She had been a virgin on their wedding night. Her experience with men was non-existent. Nick had taught her the fine points of lovemaking, and he'd taught her well enough that she loved being intimate with the man. When their bodies joined, it was as if the whole world faded into obscurity. Nothing else mattered but the joy she found cradled in his arms.

He turned to face her, somewhat startled by her declaration. He was also, she hoped, stimulated by the subject matter.

Outside the closed doors to their suite, or beyond the walls of the Grayson estate, such words would never pass her lips. But she was a modern woman who knew what she wanted, and it fell to her to make her dreams come true. It was all fine and well for her mother's generation to sit idly by while men dictated the events in their lives for them. She did not want that for herself, so she took the lead now. Emboldened by two glasses of wine with her roast beef, she wiggled her eyebrows and puckered her lips.

His grin made her heart lurch. "Oh, is that so?"

Trying hard to make the sound seem more catlike than human, she purred, "*Mmm hmm.*"

"Well, perhaps we should move this party to the bedroom. Unless you want to begin here, amidst the leftover carrots?"

He stood, pulled her into his arms and held her close. Pressing his hips suggestively against her sheer, body-hugging dinner gown, he let it be known that her forward talk had stirred him. Greatly.

It was good that she'd dressed simply. No fussy layers, just a wisp of a slip and camisole to remove. Not even more substantial undergarments, in the hope the scintillating idea of next to nothing beneath her clothes would make her irresistible.

Now, with Nick's arousal pressing hard against her hip, she smiled up at him.

Her dashing husband dropped his lips to hers, pulling her into a kiss that began tenderly but quickly turned passionate. His tongue slid into her open mouth as a rumble tore through him. She felt his desire, not only in the state of his pants but by the way his mouth ravished hers.

Lucie nipped his lower lip. Then, she ran her tongue over the spot. Pulling away, she looked up. His eyes gleamed.

"You are quite the wanton woman," he teased as he dropped his gaze to the slope of her breasts. The cut of her gown was so low the edge skimmed her nipples. It was not something to be worn where others might observe the indiscretion; she'd had the item made for her husband's eyes only.

Nick cupped one breast, running a lazy finger across its peak. It responded to his touch, pebbling beneath his skin. When he pushed her neckline aside, exposing her, she did not object.

"You are enticing, my angel. Utterly captivating. I have known that from the first instant we met. I love you, more than I can say."

He dropped a kiss on her neck, just below her earlobe. Then, he trailed a line straight down her skin, ending at the nipple he rubbed in his fingertips. When he caught her breast between his lips and ran his tongue across the hardened spot, she gasped. Heat pooled low in her body, bringing moisture to the apex of her thighs. It might not be respectable, but by God she enjoyed every moment of the attention.

A moan tore from her throat. Lucie swallowed, thankful he held her upright. Her knees wobbled, desire turning her flesh to putty.

"Nick…oh, Nick…"

Her fingers twined in his curls as he caressed her breast. She kissed his temple, sighing against his skin.

"Nick?"

"*Hmm*?"

"I…oh, I…"

He brought his gaze up to meet hers. There was no shyness between them. They had agreed never to have secrets, so she did not hesitate now.

"I want something. Desperately. Please…"

He turned serious. "Name it. Whatever your heart desires, my love, you shall have. If it is in my power to give, that is."

"It is within your power…"

"What, then?"

She held his gaze for a long moment. His eyes were the darkest brown she'd ever seen, their depths seemingly endless. Not for the first time, she thought she could drown in his beautiful eyes.

"I want a baby…please, I want a baby."

He nodded then reached down, lifted her into his arms, and strode across the room. At the doorway to their bed chamber, he paused.

"It is precisely what I want, as well. There is only one way I am aware of that will make our wish come true, my love. Only one way…"

## Chapter 8

Moonlight danced in his eyes when Nick looked over at her, sending a jolt of heat to her center.

They had the carriage to themselves and were in no hurry to make the musicale in time for the opening notes. He had instructed the driver to give them a long, lazy ride, and that was precisely what they were getting.

She leaned back against her husband. Contentment made her smile, even though no one could see the expression in the darkness. She sighed.

"That sounds like a happy noise, my dear." He spoke into her temple, his breath warm on her skin.

"It is. Quite happy."

They had a long, serious discussion, late at night after they'd sated their desire. It was the first night he was at Willowbrook in far too long. It upset him to know she was less than content with their current arrangement, and he promised to be present more and on business less. And since it was mid-Season, with so many intriguing events to attend, they decided to remain at the estate with her family rather than return to their own home. There were, after all, more people in one place over the other, and that, the enjoyment of one's friends and family, was a high point of any Season.

He had been true to his word. He spent his days riding with Lord Gregory, or attending one of the endless lawn parties that filled their afternoons. Or, he and Lucie spent any moment they could steal in their apartment, locked in a lovers' embrace.

"I'm glad." He rubbed his palm along her upper arm, just below the filmy emerald-green shawl wrapped around her shoulders. The night was warm, but a woman could not go out without the proper attire, so the shawl came along. "But you must promise me something. I absolutely demand it, Lucie."

Her husband had only ever demanded one thing from her, and that was part of their betrothal agreement. She had not strayed from the vow she made him.

"A demand? Why, that hardly seems like you. Whatever is on your mind?" She searched his gaze, but aside from the pinpricks of moonlight reflected in the dark depths, she could see nothing unusual.

"Promise me this: I will know the instant you are unhappy. I hate the thought that you were not altogether content with our marriage, that I had done something to upset you, and you did not tell me right away. I demand to know the minute I am being less than the ideal husband. You must promise."

Her heart thudded. He was a wonderful man, so kind he had agreed to marry her to save her family's reputation as well as conceal the truth about her brother's addiction. He had been selfless and loving, and had given her elderly father his word of honor that he would take care of the family estate, as well as the family that came with said property.

"Oh, no, Nick—you must never think I was unhappy. I was—"

He silenced her with a kiss. A gentle, sweet, soft kiss.

"You were unhappy with me. It is understandable." He placed a hand on her neck, cradling her head as he caressed her throat with his thumb. "It is no excuse, but I am accustomed to tending my affairs first, and am not yet used to having a personal life. My whole life, no one has cared whether I come or go, or when I return home to eat or sleep. It has always been…well, it has been a lonely life. I see that now. I am learning, Lucie. Please, promise you will not allow me to neglect you in any way whatsoever, ever again."

She nodded, the lump in her throat much too large for her to speak around. Knowing he never had a loving family was one thing; realizing the solitude of his existence was another. It hurt her that he'd ever lived thusly. The only thing she could do? Make sure he never felt acute loneliness again.

Their kiss was tender. Her lips opened to his willingly, and they deepened their passion. The carriage was closed. The driver could not peek, and the two footmen who rode the back step were facing the road behind. They were insulated, in a world of their own, and they took absolute advantage.

Lucie wore a gown with a full skirt. While it was fashionable to wear sheer, body-skimming gowns, she still favored the grander style for nights out. Now, she straddled her husband's legs, her skirts billowing out on the seat around them.

A low, deep rumble of appreciation when she reached down and undid the buttons on his trousers.

"Why, Lady Grayson," he murmured against her lips.

She broke their kiss, looked down into his eyes with the most innocent expression she could conjure given she had his member in her hand.

"Do you object?"

"Do I feel as if I object?" He thrust his steely length against her palm, a slow push that brought the butterflies in her belly alive.

She moved aside the fabric separating her skin from his. Teasing, she brushed the tip of his need against the slick of her desire. Nick swallowed a moan, so she repeated the motion, bringing him oh, so close to the place he wanted to be before slipping him just out of position.

Their passion had been playful from the very first night. She learned from him how to please a man and how to be pleased in turn. Stalling fulfillment took self-control but was worth the effort.

"Why, as a matter of fact, Nicky dearest, you don't feel objectionable at all." She moaned as she lowered herself onto him. There was nothing in heaven or on earth that could feel as incredible as being joined to one's own heart.

The motion of the carriage made short work of their passion. They laughed quietly, mindful of the servants just inches away, when it was over. Lucie lingered on her husband's lap, putting off the moment when they would be two again, rather than one.

A loud shout from the driver. Then, the horses whinnied, and the carriage ground to a halt.

The footmen hollered, their voices harsh and their words unintelligible, as chaos broke out beyond their cozy world.

Nick lifted her off him and settled her onto the seat. He fastened his trousers in haste.

"Stay here, Lucie. No matter what you hear, stay

here."

A quick brush of the lips, then he opened the door and jumped out of the carriage. He slammed the door, then was gone.

Chapter 9

The plush seats in Lord and Lady Harrison's ballroom were comfortable. The warm breeze coming from the open French doors leading to the terrace was sultry against his skin. And the seemingly endless music was mesmerizing. It took a supreme effort for Oliver to keep his eyes open. He had caught his chin falling toward his chest twice so far, and had only kept himself from embarrassment by an elbow from the woman beside him.

This time, the third, that Amy touched her skin against his evening jacket, had to be the last. He gave her a grateful nod, which she returned with a small acknowledgement. They had known each other forever so he had no fear she wouldn't keep his secret.

On the other side of Amy sat Miranda, dressed in her signature blue. Both sisters were lovely, each in her own way.

The Spencer sisters' parents were gadabouts and had never shown the ladies the love and respect they deserved. But the pair were not women to be dallied with. They would make good wives, prosperous matches and hopefully have the lives they were born to live.

There was no sense encouraging Miranda when he knew in his heart there was no spark between them. So, he was polite, as he would be to any young lady, but kept his distance.

Amy had no designs on him so she was quite safe to side beside. This past year she and an earl's son had been on the high ropes, and while they hadn't declared permanence to their friendship, the *ton* expected it be forthcoming. So, she was safe when it came to seating arrangements.

He leaned close enough to whisper. "I am going for a turn about the terrace. It is too hot by far in here. Excuse me, please."

Amy grabbed his wrist before he could rise.

"Take me with you, I beg you. I am dying from this heat—it is stifling, and if I don't get some relief, I shall surely swoon."

The lighting was dim, but Oliver looked into her face to see her cheeks were, indeed, flushed. Her eyes had a sheen, as if she might dissolve into tears if he refused.

A nod. "People may talk."

"I don't give a groat what people say. They will talk if I slide off this chair in a puddle, a victim to this close air."

His was the last seat in their row, so exiting required little effort. They did not disturb anyone with their departure, although they did garner a puzzled glance from Miranda as they rose. Oliver gave her a tiny nod, and a matching smile, to placate her.

The air on the terrace was sheer delight by comparison to the sticky, perfumed fog they left behind. Oliver followed Amy to the farthest edge of the space, where she leaned against the wide stone wall and took a deep breath. He watched as she dropped her head back, closed her eyes and smiled. She'd been so under the weather recently that it was a good sign, he thought, to see her relax.

"It is much better out here, isn't it?" Oliver was less inclined to stick to prescribed topics of conversation with the Spencer sisters. They had, after all, grown up together so there was a closeness not found with others.

Amy was equally relaxed. "Yes, much."

She glanced around them. Aside from several servants carrying refreshment trays, there were several other couples scattered about. Apparently they were not the only ones seeking fresh air.

"Are you enjoying the music? The woodwinds are especially talented, I think."

"I love music. You know that, I don't need to tell you. You've endured your fair share of evenings filled with Miranda's pianoforte accompanying my harp. The music is fine, and it is a good night for it. It's just much too warm in there for my taste." A lace fan hung from a ribbon tied around her left wrist. She used it now, moving the air near her face with a slow, careless wave. He watched a tendril, a small curl, hanging near her cheek move languorously in the artificial breeze.

"Would you like something to drink?"

A maid paused beside them, waiting while they looked over the glasses on her tray. Strawberry punch on one side, for the ladies. On the other side, port, for the gentlemen.

Amy grimaced. Averted her face and fanned more enthusiastically. He waved the servant away, concerned by the way his companion suddenly turned pale.

"Do you need to sit down?"

She did not answer right away. He watched, as

Amy swallowed. Once. Twice. Three times. A shake of her head, which sent the little curl bobbing beside her face.

"No need. I am…I am fine. Really." Her voice was shaky, and there was a glow to her that hadn't been there before the drink tray was presented.

He knew better than to believe her. Those who claimed to be fine were generally the ones who were anything but.

"You are a beautiful woman who is feeding me a faradiddle. I taste it, you know." The ploy worked, and he got a weak smile for his teasing. "My mother is quite concerned about you. Lucie is, as well. You have been not yourself for the past few weeks. Perhaps a consultation with Doctor Fairweather is in order?"

She shook her head so hard the feather tucked into the back of her upsweep flew from its place. It fluttered to the stone terrace and landed at her feet. He bent, retrieved the embellishment, and held it in his hand.

She made no move to take it from him, so he did not offer it at once. Instead, he watched as she struggled to keep her composure. It tore at his heartstrings to see her so distressed.

"I do not wish to see a doctor." The statement was softly but firmly spoken, punctuated by another brisk head shake. "No doctor."

He deferred to her, of course.

"As you wish. But truly, we are concerned. You are not yourself, not at all. And you have been ill a number of times, which is not the best way to spend your days." He searched his mind for a compelling line that might open the vault she kept locked against confidences. "And, I have noticed your, ah, companion is absent recently."

She did not look at him. "My companion?"

Oliver should have realized something was amiss when she did not meet his gaze. "Lyle Roarke. I have not seen him these past weeks…come to think of it, I have not heard one word of him from anyone. Surely, you must miss him. It seems you two have a particular fondness."

When she looked up, she stared at a point beyond his shoulder. The darkness gave way to the lights shining from the windows in the houses surrounding this one, but he did not believe she saw either light or darkness. It was as if a curtain had been drawn over her eyes. A haunted look, matching the tone in her voice.

"I have no knowledge of that man. He has not contacted me in weeks." A stifled sob, the fan stilling in front of her mouth.

He had no real experience with distressed females so he placed a hand on her shoulder in a brotherly gesture he prayed would soothe her.

"Amy, I know there is something wrong. Can't you confide in me?"

She met his gaze. Shook her head. A single tear rolled down her cheek.

"I need to leave," she whispered. "Please, take me out of here."

Chapter 10

Lights shone from nearly every window when the carriage pulled up to the front door. The ride from London had been silent, neither sister inclined to speak and Oliver more than happy to let them keep their own councils. He'd watched Amy sniff away a tear more than once. Miranda's brow was so furrowed he wondered if it might remain thusly. She had never been an expert at hiding her emotions; now her vexation was as clear as a pebble in the bottom of a bucket of water.

Miranda placed a hand on her chest and gasped as the carriage rolled to a stop. "Something is wrong—the place should be quiet at this hour."

The footman opened the door. It was difficult, but he allowed the ladies to exit before him. She was right, there could be no good reason for the manor looking like a birthday cake well past midnight.

Amy murmured, "I do hope it's not your parents. They both seemed fine when we departed. I pray nothing has changed."

They passed through the front door, not bothering to remove hats, gloves or shawls. The sound of excited voices came from the library, so they hurried to the open doorway.

Oliver strode into the room. His parents, both in their nightclothes, sat on an overstuffed settee. Father had a reassuring arm around his mother, who, with her hair plaited and hanging over her shoulder, reminded him of a younger Lucie.

Lucie and Vivian sat beside the fire. It appeared Vivian, also in her nightdress but with one of Will's overcoats draped around her shoulders, soothed his sister. Tea filled china cups on the table beside the chairs. Not one cup looked as if it had been sampled.

"Whatever is going on?" He walked into the center of the room, his gaze passing from face to face. The sisters hurried in on his heels; Miranda going to his parents' side and Amy to kneel before Lucie and Vivian. "What has happened? And why is no one asleep?"

Will and Nick were in the far corner near Father's massive oak desk conferring with two of the grounds men. When they turned to face him, he saw the reason for the night's excitement.

Nick glared at him from one eye. The other, bruised purple and swollen shut. His lip was split, and his once immaculate attire was dirty, torn, and bloodied. Blood dried on his neck and had turned his white shirt collar crimson.

His sister's weeping filled the air. She was not prone to fits of emotion, so the sound was as heart wrenching as the sight of her husband's face was shocking.

He crossed the room, placed his hands on his brother-in-law's shoulders. "Good God, man! What happened?"

Nick opened his mouth, then closed it with a grimace. A trickle of blood from the lip, where it had burst open.

Will spoke to the grounds men first. "As soon as

help arrives, allow them entrance. And Doctor Fairweather's carriage is to be admitted. But secure the grounds immediately. No one enters the estate—and make certain all men posted at the entrance are armed. Do I make myself clear?"

The two men acknowledged their assignment. They left in a hurry, without looking at anyone in the room. The front door closed so forcefully they heard the slam, something almost unheard of at Willowbrook.

Will gestured to the wide leather chair behind Lord Gregory's desk. He looked into Nick's one good eye. "Best sit down. The doctor may take a while to arrive. But the cook is on her way in with something to clean you up a bit."

Nick sat, turning away from the rest of the room. It was clear he was sparing the others the sight. It occurred to Oliver his consideration in the face of whatever had befallen him was highly admirable.

Will stood behind the chair, using his body as a shield so as to further conceal the man. Oliver stood shoulder to shoulder with him, making an even more formidable wall.

"What the hell is going on here? What happened—and where is the bastard who did this to him?"

Nick laid his head back against the leather and closed his eye. It was painful to look at him, so he turned his gaze to the man beside him.

"They were come upon by bandits on the road between here and Town. Their carriage left not ten minutes after yours did, so it is probable you passed the scoundrels on your way to the musicale." Will's hair stood on end. He plowed his fingers through it, sending his waves into an even greater mess. "They nearly killed him. And your sister, she saw it all."

Acid rose in his throat. He swallowed hard, then knelt in front of Nick, looked up into his battered face and hitched a breath. "I give you my word, I will find the ones who did this to you. And when I do, they will pay for this. I promise, brother."

Nick managed one word. "Lucie."

"She is safe. Now, let's get you upstairs." The cook and three maids entered, all bearing fresh towels, warm water, and assorted medical items. "You will be more comfortable in bed, and it will be easier to tend to your needs if you are lying down. Will, let's lift him and carry him up."

Nick protested, waving one arm as he tried to rise. He barely made it to his feet before his knees buckled. When he fell forward, they caught him.

The body knows what it needs, and the battered duke needed rest from his wounds. Blessedly, he lost consciousness so he was able to be carried without further protest. When they reached the wide staircase, servants and family trailing behind them, Will caught Oliver's gaze.

"He managed to bring one down. The footmen are both badly injured, but the driver held them off with Nick until another carriage appeared. Three men ran off, but they broke a leg on one. Bastard couldn't run so we have him in the barn."

"That is where he belongs," Oliver said. "With the other animals."

He was grateful when he heard the doctor's voice in the hallway below. Nick was milquetoast white and breathing shallowly.

The notion that Nick might not survive this assault

swept over him. Losing the man so quickly after he joined the family seemed an unimaginable horror, but life had taught him that not all horrors lived in nightmares. Some, like the atrocity unfolding this very night, ventured out of the shadows.

He prayed the doctor was in time to save Nick.

Chapter 11

Sleep was an elusive bedfellow, in many rooms and for every inhabitant of the manor house, as well as the Fulbright Cottage. None could get the images of a battered man from their minds, or his precarious hold on life from their nightmares.

Breakfast did not take place in the dining room. It did not occur on the flower-decked terrace, either. Anyone with an appetite took the meal in their own room. Most trays were returned untouched.

Oliver sent his parents to their rooms right after the doctor arrived. And he had the doctor check on them when he had finished with Nick's care. Neither Lord nor Lady Gregory resisted his taking charge. In fact, they relinquished the position without any fuss whatsoever.

He had been awake the whole night. The groundskeepers had reported more than once. No uninvited persons attempted to enter the estate, but he still kept armed guards stationed at the main gate as well as the small roads leading into the surrounding countryside. Willowbrook would not be invaded. It was despicable enough that one of their own had been assaulted already.

The prisoner received care from the doctor, after Nick, his parents, then the carriage men, were attended to.

When Doctor Fairweather advised the prisoner be moved from the stable, Oliver refused. He would not shelter the man in his home. Had the estate kept pigs, he would place the criminal in the pigpen.

He'd met with the law three times already. They had found an abandoned firearm near the spot where the incident had taken place. It belonged to one of the footmen, who had already disclosed he had discharged it one time only, in an effort to kill the man who was choking Lord Grayson. Oliver was torn between applauding the man's efforts and slapping him for endangering Nick. Had the shot struck the duke instead of the assailant, the day could be much more somber by far than it already was.

Blood at the scene indicated that at least one of the robbers had been shot. There was a city-wide alert for anyone who turned up with an unexplainable gunshot wound.

He had not allowed the physician to leave, and the man had not been inclined to do so anyhow. He had the maid show him to an upstairs room near Lucie and Nick's apartment. Presumably, he had checked on the patient through the night.

Oliver stretched, his back and shoulders stiff from sitting in the same position for so long. His father's desk, a huge piece of furniture, was the perfect height for placing his legs upon. His ankles crossed, he leaned back and stared at the ceiling.

The weight of the position of Lord of the Manor was heavier than he imagined it might be. How had his father carried it for so long? And his ancestors? Didn't anyone grow weary of the burden?

And that is why the English aristocracy have sons,

he thought. Dash it all—even a son could be overwhelmed by the magnitude of so many looking to him for answers. And he had none to give, which was the worst part. This morning he was no closer to learning who had assaulted the carriage carrying his sister and her husband than he had been the night before.

Will walked into the room. He was, as was his way, perfectly starched and turned out.

"Good morning." He claimed a leather arm chair on the other side of the desk. His gaze took in Oliver's stockinged feet, wrinkled evening wear and bloodshot eyes. "You look dreadful."

"I feel pretty damn dreadful." Never one to resist a chance to get in a good-natured poke, he added, "But you look as if you just stepped off the pages of the *Gentleman's Quarterly.*"

Adjusting his tie, Will smiled. "Well, my wife does take rather good care of me. And my clothes."

"Did she ever discover the Bond Street beverage, Lord Greendick?" He chuckled at the memory. It was barely two days past, yet it seemed a lifetime ago.

"Indeed, she did. And, she was not at all happy about the unpleasant odor. At this point in her impending motherhood, odors seem to be very important." He shook his head. "What can I say? I don't understand it, but when she turns green at the whiff of something disagreeable, I open a window."

"Smart fellow. Well, in the end you will both be happy."

"And you will be an uncle."

"A very proud uncle." Oliver already wondered how to best spoil the little one. Unbeknownst to either

Will or Vivian, there was already a sum of money in trust for the babe. But that, like so many other things in life, was something best kept until the proper time.

Now was not the proper time.

He scrubbed a hand over his cheek. The bristles rasped against his palm, the sound loud in his ear. Before long, he'd have to get cleaned up.

But not yet. Waving to the tray a maid had brought just before his assistant's arrival, he asked, "Tea? Hot chocolate? A scone? Or has Vivian fed you already?"

The other man reached for the tray. He poured a cup of tea, added some cream, and then handed the cup across the desk. He took it, as well as the blueberry scone that was sliced and buttered before being pushed across the blotter toward him. He hadn't thought he was hungry, but the food looked appealing.

Will served himself. They ate without speaking. So close they didn't feel compelled to fill the silence with words, they enjoyed the light repast.

Finally. "Any news of Nick? Vivian is sick with worry over him—and over Lucie, too. She will be here in short order, I am sure of it. She would have accompanied me, but I refused to allow it. She needs her rest, so I sent her back to bed with the promise she not move for at least one hour."

He checked his watch. With a rueful smile, he pushed the watch back into his waistcoat pocket.

"It is now five minutes past the prescribed hour. I have no doubt my wife is, at this very minute, dressing."

"You are probably right. And, it is a good thing that she comes over. While I have guards at the gates, I would feel better if we were all in one place for the time being. Until we solve this mess, anyhow. And, Lucie must be completely done in. It will be a calming influence to have Vivian, with her soothing violet eyes, nearby."

"Yes, they are rather soothing, aren't they? But about Nick? How is he faring?"

The truth was difficult to admit. "The doctor says that if he makes it through the next two or three days, he has a chance of survival. The worst is, he was pummeled about the back so dramatically that his internal organs may be damaged. He is…good God, I can barely say it, but he is bleeding. From…"

"No."

"Yes. If he lives, who knows if he will be able to be a real husband to my sister. The doctor said as much, but I will not tell anyone else. Will, this is between us. No one must know that we may have the last Lord Grayson lying upstairs, hanging on to life by a thread. No one."

"You have my word, of course. My absolute word."

Chapter 12

Amy did not imagine anyone would be about when she crept down the wide front staircase. She had been up and down the steps so many times, she knew to avoid the seventh step from the bottom because of the squeaky tread.

With the horrid turn of events last night, everyone should still be resting after their late nights. She hadn't gotten to sleep until well after midnight, but vivid dreams and a queasy tummy stole her rest. It was just as well; this day's errand required no witnesses.

Her hand was on the door latch when she heard voices emanating from the library. There, too, she had spent many hours, so she saw clearly in her mind's eye one man behind the desk, and the other in the comfortable leather visitor chair. She preferred the window seat to any other spot in the large room, but it seemed highly unlikely either man would choose that secluded nook.

The last thing she wanted to do was eavesdrop, but there was no way to avoid it. Her only concern was escape—undetected—but when she heard the words "hanging by a thread" she gasped. And, the house being so quiet and she being suddenly startled, she forgot that the door hinge squeaked. Loudly. Opening the door too quickly brought about the annoying—and revealing—sound.

Will appeared in the library doorway. He lifted his eyebrows in surprise before regaining his composure.

"Good morning, Miss Spencer. It is rather early to be up and about, isn't it?"

Before she could reply, Oliver stood beside him in the doorway. They were night and day, the assistant starched and pressed, and the duke done to a turn.

Even in his stocking feet, Oliver was a full head taller than the other man. And despite his dishevelment he looked every inch the peer. He frowned when he saw her.

"Are you well? It seems you should be abed, considering last night's unfortunate excitement." He dashed a hand over his cheek, then through his hair.

He went around the other man and walked to where she stood. The front door hung open, until he closed it.

"I am fine, thank you." She looked from one to the other; neither looked at all rested. "Is there any word on Nick's condition? I have prayed all night he is already being restored to health."

She could not imagine how Lucie must feel right now. The ordeal itself was bad enough but to have one's husband so thoroughly beaten was beyond understanding. And she had heard the melee, seen the blood…

Amy shuddered.

Oliver placed a calming hand on her shoulder. "We are all praying. He made it through the night, and that is a fine start. Speaking of starts, where are you off to so early this morning?"

Lies. Being enamored with Lyle Roarke had taught her the finer side of lying, not that she condoned the practice but when forced into a corner she had become skilled at conjuring a half-truth. It was the way of the world, Lyle had said, to bend the rules to suit one's purposes.

It was wrong, she knew that. But if she told the truth about so many things, the repercussions would be endless. And her ruination would bring the Spencer name low—too low. It was all a woman had—her name, which gave her a place in polite society if she were at all fortunate. Losing that place? Not if a bit of lying could prevent it.

"I could not sleep so I think a walk will do me good. Some fresh air, and all that. If you will excuse me—"

"I cannot allow that, Amy. Until we discern what happened last night, everyone needs to be mindful of the danger." Oliver sounded weary, but firm. "You cannot go walking about by yourself."

"My lady's maid is occupied. I cannot pull her from her duties. And, we are all mindful of the danger—but it was on the road beyond the gates, not in the gardens. I am certain I will be perfectly safe." The pool of lies she told grew every time she opened her mouth. Soon she would drown in it if she didn't take care.

"The danger is on the road, always, but until I am certain this was a random attack rather than a targeted endeavor, we will take precautions." He turned to Will, who had been standing near the staircase listening. "I will accompany Miss Spencer on her morning constitutional. We will take a turn about Mother's rose garden, so if I am needed, that is where I shall be."

\*\*\*\*

A man knew when his company was not wanted,

but Oliver did not care. If Amy—or any female, for that matter—stubbornly refused to see it was safer to remain indoors until matters were sorted out, she would get a bodyguard. One life hanging in the balance was one life too many. And if feathers got ruffled, well, that was fine with him, too. Feathers eventually smoothed, even on the pluckiest birds.

She ignored him as they walked toward the rose garden. It did not matter; just being outdoors cleared his head. The long night left him with a dull ache in his skull. Had he been inclined to take one of the doctor's fixatives he might chase it away sooner rather than later, but there was no pain great enough to lure him into taking medicinal draughts.

"You do not need to do this. I am perfectly capable of walking on my own." Her voice turned from stubborn to sweet. She looked up at him and batted her eyelashes. "Why, you were probably with me when I took my first steps. This is silly. You are a busy man, and I am keeping you. Really, I can manage to stroll without your attention."

She had a smile that would melt another man's heart, but he had seen how well Amy's machinations worked on members of his sex. He had watched her ply men with ego-inflating phrases borne on that sweet, lilting voice many, many times—and all to her great success.

He was not as prone to falling for her sweetness. Not that he didn't appreciate a lady's honeyed talk, but he wasn't going to be swatted aside like some annoying insect.

"Oh, I am well aware of just how capable you are, both in the walking and dancing departments."

They reached the closest rose garden and took a turn near his favorite blooms. Yellow and peach, filling the air with their captivating perfume, these were the roses he had picked for his mother when he was a child. The thorns were deadly sharp, but the flower made the danger worth the risk.

Oliver stopped beside a heavily laden plant. Flowers dripped from the stems in such profusion they nearly concealed the greenery beneath. The gardeners shaped these bushes into mounds, so they looked like yellow hills. He chose a bloom, bending the stem until it broke. Using his fingernail, he cleared the stem of thorns.

Bowing, he presented his companion the rose. She accepted with a sigh, placing it near her nose. A deep whiff, and a smile.

"Thank you." She took another whiff, looking lost in thought.

"A sovereign for what lurks behind those eyes."

She did not look up. "Nothing…"

He did not rush her, choosing instead to feign nonchalance and sniff several blooms on the bush. It was large, so the flowers hung at his shoulders. The garden itself was maze-like, with long, meandering lanes between rows of scent and color. An artists' dream, affording countless inspiring views.

"A shared burden is half as heavy." He did not look at her, and said the words in a gentle tone.

"I don't think I can share this."

Oliver looked up. She still stared at the rose, so he placed a finger beneath her chin and lifted her face. When he met her gaze, he saw so much sorrow it nearly broke his own heart. All the years he had an association with the sisters, he had admired Amy's independence. She was fun and adventurous, always smiling and determined not to allow their lack of parental guidance to bring her down. She was very dissimilar to her clinging, nervous sister and that appealed to him.

But now, with the tired, worrisome frown on her pretty face, she barely looked like the woman he knew.

"You can share it. And who better, than someone who has known you for so many years? Why, we are practically related."

She tried to look away, but he leaned closer. The rose, held before her in one white-gloved hand, brushed the front of his jacket.

"Oliver, I cannot…there is nothing…oh!"

Tears came in a rush, so he folded her in his arms and held her close. The moment was entirely unexpected, and had anyone witnessed their improper behavior it would create a scandal. But society be damned—he could not let her suffer without offering a caring shoulder to lean upon.

He smoothed a hand over her back, soothing her the way he would a weeping child. Words eluded him, so he remained silent, hoping Amy would speak when she was able. The tears subsided to sniffles, then tapered off, and still they stood. It was several moments before he realized the woman in his arms had ceased crying, but seemed in no hurry to leave his embrace.

It was completely unexpected when it occurred to him that he did not mind holding her in his arms. He had never thought to do so, but it was a pleasant turn of events.

## Chapter 13

Amy tried to concentrate on her needlework, but she was making a bumblebroth of things. The sampler, with its cheery birds and butterfly border, dangled tangled threads of every color of the rainbow. It just showed that concentration when wielding a needle and thread was somewhat necessary.

She put the fabric aside. It would take more patience than she possessed today to unsnarl the mess.

Miranda had been staring at the same page of her book for an hour. She knew, because the vellum pages whispered when turned, and there had been no whispering since the book was opened.

Vivian sat beside Lady Gregory on a wide, comfortable side chair. It was large enough to accommodate at least three women, or one man and a woman, so the two had lots of room to spread their sewing accessories on either side of them. An equally wide footstool kept their toes off the floor.

As was her norm, the older woman worked an intricate pattern on brocade. Many of the chair seats in the rooms of the manor were covered with the fine needlework she created. A lifetime of stitchery produced countless beautiful mementos. She steadfastly pulled thread through fabric, her motions precise.

Vivian glanced at the older woman many times as she worked the baby garment in her hands. Having been employed in a Stropshire dress shop, bringing fabric to life was second nature to her. Today's little robins' egg blue bunting was getting hearts and swirls around its outer edges. The colorful splashes raised the item from functional to fun.

Only Lucie was absent. She hadn't left her husband's side once. The doctor was still present, going between the coachmen, the prisoner and the duke. His expression was somber, and he did not share details with the women, so they were left to wonder what went on.

Small talk, she thought. That is what we need, something to take everyone's mind off the sad situation.

"Ah, Vivian…that is a very pretty bunting. Actually, all the baby things are so lovely. Have you made many before now, or is this your first foray into the newborn-clothing business?"

As she knew she would, the mother-to-be smiled when asked about anything related to the baby. She put her handwork down, ran a palm across her middle and sighed.

"I once made a christening gown. It was two years ago, and the mother did not give a groat what the gown looked like. Oh, but that was an interesting commission."

Miranda looked up with a puzzled frown. "But if she didn't care, didn't that leave you free to make whatever you pleased? I would think it would be simpler if no one had any definite rules for what they did—or didn't—want."

"Ah, but I did not say no one cared what the gown looked like." She kept a protective hand on her tummy. Amy watched and wondered how it must feel to know—for certain—there was a child within your body. She had so many questions, yet no one to ask. "There was, you see, a grandmother…and this lady was undeniably one of the most difficult customers I ever had. She had so many ideas about that one teeny, tiny gown, it was nearly impossible to get every detail into the fabric."

Lady Gregory smiled. "The older we get, the more demanding we become. Is that what you are saying, dear?"

Vivian laughed. "Not at all. I'm just saying that this grandmother was so excited to welcome that baby that she made it almost a trial to construct a gown suitable for the big moment."

Amy was glad she had begun the conversation. Tension eased, and idle chatter was a distraction.

She had to know. "Did you make the gown? And was the grandmother satisfied?"

A quick nod. "I did—and she was. There were many good points to her long list of details, so the gown itself turned out very well, if I do say so. The mother still did not seem interested, even when they retrieved the garment from the shop, but the grandmother made up for it. She was over the moon, just so happy her daughter was expecting and almost too eager by far to put the baby in the new gown. It was a touching moment…"

The thought that a mother could care at all what her grown daughter might do stabbed Amy's heart. She glanced at Miranda, who was too preoccupied with something to realize they had been denied the caring mothering others took as their due.

Maybe she wouldn't be in such a predicament now

if her mother had paid them some mind. But, she could not fob off her own poor choices on someone else. No, she was the only one responsible for the trouble at hand. Accountability was a tiresome subject, but the facts were the facts.

"Is that the only baby garment, then?" Miranda gestured to the fabric in Vivian's lap. "Aside from this collection, that is?"

"Yes, that's all. And now, sweet things for our own baby. Why, I can hardly believe it is true." Lady Gregory reached over and patted her shoulder, and Vivian reached up to catch the other woman's hand. They sat, holding hands and smiling, a brightness in the room that had not been present just a short while earlier.

"It is true, my dear. I remember, though, how exciting it is to expect an addition. It seems only yesterday I sewed little rompers and sleep dresses for Oliver. Then, for Lucie. It is a time in a woman's life when the rest falls away and your concentration is on the life growing within you. It will never be the same, the life you lead following these days, so cherish the moments you have with your husband. They are soon to be invaded—a wonderful, blessed invasion, but an invasion nonetheless."

When Vivian rubbed her midsection, Amy's own tummy flipped. Then it flopped. A sudden wave of nausea rolled over her. It happened so frequently these past two weeks she had almost learned to accept the unpleasant sensations. Almost. Perspiration turned her clammy, lack of sleep left her less able to deal with the changes within her, and she did the unthinkable. For the second time in as many hours, tears slid from her eyes.

"Sister, what is wrong?" Miranda hadn't been so self-absorbed she failed to see her sibling's distress. She put her book aside, stood and rushed to Amy's chair. "Dearheart, what is it? Are you unwell again?"

"That's it. We need to call for the doctor. He is just upstairs—" Vivian rose and would have left the room, but Amy would not allow it.

"No! Please—I am…I-I-I…"

She could not speak.

Her sister knelt and pulled her into her arms. The sudden burst of sibling affection brought all reserves crashing down, and she buried her face on the blue shoulder offered her and wept.

The others murmured, but she did not pay them any attention. They could guess all they wanted, but none would fathom what the problem was. She could not believe it herself, so no one else would suspect.

The truth was hers alone to bear.

She heard Oliver through her sobs when he entered the room. His usual style, all manly bluster invading the female sewing circle, made his voice louder than anyone's soft suppositions.

"Good morning, ladies. Mother, I hate to disturb you, but I have a question about one of your maids. Bridget, her name is. I am wondering—oh! Good heavens, I am sorry for being so insensitive. Whatever is wrong with Amy?"

She looked up and met Oliver's gaze. He had changed and was a dashing figure in a charcoal gray striped suit. His white shirt, bright beneath the dark jacket and his black Hessian boots polished to a high shine. By comparison, she felt wholly bedraggled.

But, she did not look away. His tone gentled.

"Amy, why so sad?"

She sniffed. Why, indeed? If he only knew, he would not gaze so kindly upon her.

And, as she looked into the eyes that were so filled with care and concern, it occurred to her that Miranda had been wise from the beginning. Oliver was a good, compassionate man. He was handsome, well-bred and had a heart for those in distress. Why hadn't she seen it before?

It mattered not. She had chosen flash over substance, and the flash of a lesser earl's dalliance would forever color her view of the world. Moreover, it might very well change her position in it.

Amy rose, wiped her cheeks on the backs of her hands. She smoothed her skirt, then looked to Lady Gregory.

Her voice did not fail her, as she feared it might. "I am sorry. I must be more tired than I realized, after last night's events. Please, excuse me. I need to rest."

"Of course, my dear." The older woman was sympathetic, but her eyes told the tale. She discerned the truth, and now that her secret was out, Amy would not be able to remain in polite company for much longer.

She made herself walk when she felt compelled to run. The room seemed bigger than ever, and it felt as if it took forever to cross from her chair to the hallway. It was all an illusion, of course…as so much of life was. Merely an illusion, all of it.

Chapter 14

Doctor Fairweather was not a young man. He had brought both Oliver and Lucie into the world. His care had gotten them through childhood illnesses, his parents' old age infirmities, and now his skill was bringing Nick from the brink of death back to the land of the living. He had seen it all, lived through more than most and knew well enough to keep it all to himself. Had he told tales, he could have kept the entire city entertained, but he was wise enough to keep the details of his medical confidences locked away.

Now, he sat back in the wide leather seat in his quarters across from the Grayson apartment and stared up with a wide-eyed look of disbelief.

"Surely you cannot mean to question the man now? I gave him a tranquilizer for the pain. He will not make a competent showing for himself. It is not fair to press him now, when he is not in full control."

"I do not care about fairness." Oliver sat in a matching chair but kept to the edge of the seat. No time to linger, but persuasion was better done at eye level. "He was not fair when he nearly killed my sister's husband. I will get the truth from him, whether it comes from a laudanum haze or clear thinking, I do not care. I just want to know if you learned anything when you attended him. Did he say anything I should know?"

Like the rest of the manor, the room was furnished

in excellent taste and wonderfully welcoming and comfortable. If the conversation was a pleasant one, it would be the perfect setting. But neither man enjoyed the topic so the moment was not at all pleasing.

"He did not say much. Well, not much that made sense." Doctor Fairweather stroked the closely-cut white beard on his thin chin. He pulled it absently, his mind on the man and his impressions.

"What did he say? Anything at all, however silly it might seem, could give us a hint. I just want to find those responsible for this. You understand."

"Of course I understand. It is just that I don't think he really said much of anything, Oliver. A lot of screaming, as I set the leg. And he did say, more than once, that it wasn't his idea. Stopping the carriage—he insisted it wasn't his fault or his idea."

Oliver considered this information, then discarded it. It did not matter much whose idea it had been. It just mattered that he find all responsible and make them pay for their actions.

"Anything else?"

The doctor shook his head. "Nothing. I don't make a habit of listening to criminals when I tend them. And, between us? I don't save a gentle touch for scoundrels."

Will had little stomach for aggressive action, so Oliver did not ask him to be present when he questioned the prisoner. He went to the stable alone. And, he did not alert any of the stable hands to his presence when he arrived.

His timing was excellent. Most of the stalls were empty, the horses having been taken outdoors to enjoy the fine day. Some were being curried, an ongoing task with so many animals. Others were being checked or refitted for shoes. Willowbrook's horseflesh was a substantial investment and attended to accordingly.

Stalls lined both sides of the large building. It smelled of wood, hay, horse and grain. Oliver pulled the sweet scent into his lungs as he made his way to the last stall on the left-hand side. The end stall was different than the others. Iron bars rose from high walls and attached to a dropped plank ceiling. The only way in or out, a wide, heavy oak door.

A large padlock secured the cell. He looked in through the tiny window set high in the wood. The space was large, but there wasn't much to see.

He slid the key home, turned, and felt the tumblers slide before he removed the lock from the hasp and threaded it onto a length of chain hanging from a hook on the nearby wall. Just before he opened the door, he took a spare piece of chain, looping it around a fist.

The door swung open on silent hinges. The man lay immobile in a nest of hay. He hadn't been cleaned up, aside from the place where his leg had been cared for, so he was still bloodied and filthy.

The space was not like the others. Square. Larger, with anchors for chains secured to the walls. It was where they brought the desperately sick animals, and if needed, sedate or secure them so they would not injure themselves. It was generally empty but now proved the ideal jail space.

Oliver swung the chain in a wide arc over the form, smacking it hard against the plank wall just a foot above the sleeping man's head. He woke instantly, tried to sit up, and was yanked backward by the chain attaching his wrist to the wall behind him.

Slapping against the hay and wooden wall, the man

howled in pain.

Heavy and non-negotiable, the cold steel against his palm mirrored his disposition. Oliver swung the chain in a new arc, acting as if he were about to send it into the man's head, but calculating so he missed the screaming figure by inches.

It wouldn't do to squish the bug while it might still be of some use.

"What were you doing last night on the highway? And who were you with?"

"I weren't doing nothing, I swear!" The captive scrambled, a one-legged crabwalk, back against the wall. His bad leg stuck out in front of him. It made for a rather comical scene—had Oliver been of a mind to be amused. He wasn't, so he swung the chain again. This time, he hit the wall close to the man's bad leg.

"Stop, please!"

"What were you doing last night?"

"I beg you—I'm sorry. I won't never do that again—please forgive me, I—"

"I'm the wrong man to beg forgiveness from. I'm not the one you killed."

Stretching the truth with a thief? Hardly counted as a lie.

The man's eyes looked like dinner plates. He wasn't a big man and did not look particularly healthy. Not well-fed, for certain. His clothes were near tatters. Deep hollows beneath his eyes and a number of rotting teeth told their own tale.

"No! I didn't kill anyone—it was just a hold up, they said. No one would get hurt, they said. Get the goods, sell 'em and..."

He wiped his free hand over his face, covering his

eyes with dirty, twisted fingers.

Still, Oliver did not take pity upon him. He hadn't shown any mercy when he assaulted Nick, so why should he expect any now?

But, he had to know. "And what?"

The prisoner did not answer right away. His hand shook where it hid his eyes and then his shoulders began to convulse. A sob, so wretched and terrible it managed to touch Oliver's heart.

More gently, yet still firm, he prodded, "And what? What did they say you would do after you sold the things you planned to steal?"

A gulp. Then, a palm across each eye to wipe the moisture away. The man managed to meet his gaze. "Eat—and food for my children, too. A man will do terrible things when he's hungry. He will do even more terrible things when he sees his children starving." A deep, shuddering breath. "But I swear, I never meant to hurt no one. I never meant to take a man's life, I swear I didn't. All I wanted? Food for my little ones."

## Chapter 15

Many of the so-called ladies' arts were difficult for Amy. They always had been, despite the suitably proficient teachers her absent parents had provided for their daughters. While her sister had applied herself, hoping to garner parental attention with her excellence, Amy had been less compliant. She rebelled, in her own way, by not putting her best effort forward on most of their lessons. Especially the ones regarding a lady's role in a household. It was clear to her from a young age that if their mother was an example of how a lady of the manor was expected to behave, she didn't want any of it.

Her stitchery was passable but would never be held up as a fine example. She sang, but just barely. The pianoforte's keys took a beating every time she put her fingers on them, although most of the time, if the piece were not too complicated, she could muddle through. Her skills on the dance floor were adequate enough, even with regard to the French cotillion. It was, everyone admitted, the most infuriating dance, all intricate steps and turns. But by some stroke of good luck, dancing had come without effort.

The place she excelled was with a canvas and paints. Her watercolors were dreamy, intuitive pieces that made admirers stop and ponder. There was such realism in her still life scenes with oils that the fruit and flowers seemed to invite tasting and sniffing. Her portrait work was high quality, even the miniatures. But the real joy was landscape paintings, especially when the view came with a pleasing aroma.

She had hidden herself in amongst the yellow rosebushes, leaving a canopy of foliage behind her so she was concealed from the manor's east windows. Her easel, folding chair, and paint box soothed her soul, and the image coming to life across the white canvas took her mind off all her troubles.

That is, if she concentrated on the pergola dripping with rose canes. It stood at the end of the row, a riot of pink and lavender. It was not formal and brought a feeling of careless abandon that she tried to capture. She, Miranda, and Lucie had played beneath the pergola when they were children. It had been a perfect hiding spot from nannies and even Oliver.

She sighed, looking at the canvas. The pergola, flowers, and grassy space beyond were all created in paint. The colors were right, varying hues of pink, lavender, green and buttercup yellow. Clouds, fat and white, sailed across a soft blue sky. It was all there, but it did not move her the way it should have. The picture was lifeless. Flat. Not as good as she ordinarily produced.

She tossed her brush into the water cup so hard drops splayed across a lower corner of the scene. "Damn it!" Now it was even worse, with watery tints sliding into the grassy section.

"My, my…"

She turned, knocking the easel with her elbow and splashing her toes with the painty water.

Oliver looked as pleased with himself as he had

when he'd found them hiding here as children. Only now he was much more handsome, not at all growing-boy exuberance but self-assured lord of the manor.

"Such language, my dear. Wherever did you pick that up?" He took a step closer, standing at her shoulder and grinning down at her.

Craning her neck back to meet his gaze was not at all comfortable so she let it travel down the length of the man. He wore a light gray suit, sparkling white shirt and a trimly-tied cravat the color of ripe grapes. It took a certain kind of man to pull off that color, but he wore it well.

She shook her head. "Why, whatever do you mean? You know who taught me to speak that way. You didn't think we weren't listening when you chatted with your chums, did you? Oh, we all learned to talk a blue streak from dear Lucie's divine older brother."

Divine. Had she just said that? Her intention had been to jest, not flatter.

Damage already done, she thought. What's another man with an inflated ego?

He threw his head back and laughed. "Divine? Good lord, that is a stretch—unless my sister has another brother I am not aware of. Oh, you do amuse me."

She removed the palette from the folding seat beside hers and gestured. As she dropped the tool to the grass, Oliver sat. The tiny seat disappeared beneath his masculine form, but he seemed comfortable.

"I am glad I amuse someone. So, why are you sneaking up on me?"

"It is hardly sly to stroll one's gardens, is it? Had you not been so intent on scaring the birds with your colorful language you might have heard me."

A pair of wrens landed on the pergola. Immediately they began to sing, the female's warble louder and longer than the male's song.

"Just like humans, those birds." He raised one eyebrow, and she recognized his intent to tease.

Rising to his bait, a long-standing habit, she asked, "How so?"

"Oh, can't you hear? The woman is doing all the talking, and every time he attempts to tell his side of the story, she shushes him with another long rebuttal."

Oliver's grin dared her to refute him, so she smiled prettily and played along. It was much less tedious, speaking with an old friend, than contemplating her affairs.

"Well, it certainly does seem that way. But, perhaps she must get the words in while she can." They watched as the male took flight, leaving the female singing after him. She, too, flapped away, following her mate in sudden feathery silence. "There you have it. She had to speak while she could, because he was already planning to leave her behind. Just like a man..." Her voice caught. Horrified she might cry, she leaned down for the palette.

"You paint beautifully, you know. You always have."

Oliver's tone was kind, his words gentle. She gathered her emotions and turned a critical eye on the piece. The water spots were hardly noticeable and now that they were dry were readily fixed. She took the brush, shook it toward the grass, and dipped it in the green paint.

"That is a very nice thing to say." She feathered the

green in, covering the spots so well they were lost to her brush strokes.

"It is the truth."

Amy finished attending to the grass. She put the brush back into the water cup—carefully this time—and placed the paint palette on the ground again. She turned to face him.

"You have always been kind. Even when we were children, you were never one of those mean boys who pulled hair or put frogs in unexpected places. I always appreciated that."

He put his elbows on his knees, leaned forward and clasped his hands. A smile, then a shrug which pulled his jacket tight over his wide shoulders. She remembered how it felt to be carried in his arms, how much strength came from those shoulders.

"I was older. It did not seem kind to torture you ladies. Also, Father kept a close eye on me, and I knew that if I did not act the role of a duke's son, there would be payment due when he learned what I was up to. So, it was not difficult to behave like a gentleman."

It was not a conscious thought that brought her hand up to cover her heart, but a response to the sharp stabbing between her breasts. Her heart lurched, and she held her breath for a moment.

A comforting hand, closing the distance between them. He put it on her back, bringing warmth and reassurance where a chill had just shot up her spine.

"Are you unwell again?"

She shook her head, the absolute opposite of what she wanted to do. But how to ever admit her heartache? Or the fear that turned her cold?

"No, I'm not. I'm fine, really."

"You look as if you've seen a ghost."

It was an act of supreme determination that pulled her lips upward. Smiling in the face of humiliation and fear was not effortless, but she did it.

"No ghost. Just…" How to explain without fibbing too terribly?

Another man would have let the topic drop. He would have commented again on her painting. On the birds. On the scent of roses that filled the air surrounding them. Another man would have done all that—and more, even—to not have an unfortunate conversation with a woman.

Oliver Gregory was not "another man" by any means. He ran a palm down her back, gentling her with the compassionate touch while he encouraged her confidence.

"Just what? You know you can talk with me, don't you? I would not even divulge what you share to the queen herself. I promise, Amy."

Promise. The word held such high hopes. Raised a woman's heart to soar in skies she had only imagined were real.

So much rode on the seven short letters, it was almost criminal to casually utter them.

Because some things were not real, and some intentions were not kind, and there were moments that did not warrant using the word when the only promise behind its utterance was a lie. It was a lesson she had already learned—and one she did not intend to forget.

"Don't make promises you can't keep." She sounded bitter, even to her own ears. Experience colored her tone. Loneliness, despair, and broken trust made a woman harder than she should ever be.

"I don't. You can trust me." He did not remove his hand, although it stopped moving and lay across her shoulders. "Please, tell me what is wrong. We can fix it together, no one need ever know what we are up to. But I need you to talk with me—share your unhappiness so we can turn that frown into a smile."

She was tempted. Oh, so very tempted. To just lay the burden down, not to be the only soul in existence who knew the secrets of her traitorous heart.

But a man's promise was worthless. She didn't know much at this point, but she knew that.

"There is no unhappiness to share. I am fine, really."

"Those who say they are fine are generally the ones who are furthest from it. After a lifetime of friendship, you cannot confide in me? Even after I have given you my word to keep your secrets?" The sadness in his eyes almost made her capitulate. But, he was, sad eyes or not, a man.

And there was no good to come of trusting a man.

"I have no secrets, Oliver. I promise."

## Chapter 16

"We have been sitting about like bumps on logs for too many days. We need to get out, even if just for an afternoon drive. A picnic, even. Something—anything—just a diversion." Lady Gregory set the gilt-edged china cup on its saucer with an uncharacteristic clatter. "It is entirely too much to be imprisoned in one's own home when the weather is this beautiful."

Her husband did not look up from his toast and jam. He had heard too many breakfast decrees to pay this one much attention.

Amy and Miranda both turned their heads toward their hostess. It was, after all, the only polite thing to do. Neither, however, commented.

Oliver realized his mother's elegant verbal foot-stomp was aimed his way, and as such he did not have the option of not replying. He swallowed the last of his eggs and toast, touched his linen napkin to his lips and looked around. Not at his mother, seated at the far end of the wrought-iron, glass top table, but at the view from the terrace.

The property was really quite attractive. Aside from the rose garden, kitchen gardens, greenhouse, fruit orchards, and various creeks and lakes forming hidden havens, there was a Folly as well as several quaint cottages. Rolling fields, riding trails, croquet lawns...there was beauty in abundance. Far more than any park offered.

It seems one should be satisfied with what is right beneath one's nose, he thought.

Tossing his napkin onto his empty plate, he looked up and addressed his mother. Dressed in a delicate mint green morning gown, she looked as fresh as one of the daisies growing in profusion from the terra cotta pots lining the wide stone steps leading onto the grass. She seemed much more fragile than was the case, a simple illustration of the fact that judging a book by its cover was unwise.

Especially when the book scowled.

"Mother, Lucie and Nick are in no shape to be run about. You know that."

"*Hmmph!*"

Uh oh. That sound was one she borrowed from her husband and used only when particularly vexed.

"It is the truth," he insisted.

"Don't try to tangle me in truths. We both know that whether or not the rest of us are here, those two will never know. They are comfortable in their apartment, and the good doctor is keeping a close watch on Nick's progress. So, running them about, as you put it, is not at issue here."

"What is the issue, then?"

The others looked from one to the other, a ping pong match played with words rather than a ball over a dining table. If he hadn't been so frustrated in the face of such female stubbornness, he would have laughed. They did look silly.

"Why, it is clear as the nose on your face, I would think. We cannot expect to be kept imprisoned indefinitely."

"You are not imprisoned. And it is not indefinite—merely until we discover and apprehend the others involved in the highway robbery."

"We are right in Season, and if we cannot go about and socialize…well, that certainly does feel like imprisonment." She furrowed her brow, directed the next to her husband. He still worked on his toast and seemed content to let the conversation swirl on without any effort on his part. "Your father must have some feelings on the matter. Don't you, Dear?"

Conversation stilled. Lord Gregory looked longingly at his last triangle of toast but with a resigned sigh, wiped his fingertips and left the toast on his plate. He met his wife's penetrating stare.

Then, he turned to Oliver.

"Certainly we can allow your mother and the ladies some latitude, can't we?" He gazed at his wife, gave her a tiny smile, and continued. "It does not seem fair to cage such beautiful butterflies, son. A ride to Town, a turn about the park…what harm can come of that?"

Women might be the gentler sex but men knew when to bow to their graces.

"None, we hope." Oliver turned to his mother, whose frown had turned to a smile in a heartbeat. "We shall take a second carriage with guards to follow the first. And if—"

"We shall take the barouche." Lady Gregory raised her hands, palms upward, to the sky. The morning was bright and light with a promise of more to come. "It is too lovely to be closed in a horrid, stuffy carriage."

There was not a single carriage on the grounds that was either horrid or stuffy, but it was futile to point that out. So he didn't. Recognizing defeat, he nodded.

"As you wish. The barouche, but with a carriage in front of it as well as one behind."

"But—"

He did the wholly improper and cut off his own mother with a firm shake of his head.

"It is the only way you and the ladies are getting to Town, Mother. I will not take chances with those I love. Until the conclusion of this near-fatal event is at hand, we shall all be mindful of the threat."

The mention of the word "love" brought a small giggle from Miranda, but he did not acknowledge it. Someday the woman would find another to catch her fancy. He prayed that day was imminent, but until it was, he would not encourage her to attempt to forge a connection that would never be made.

Amy turned to him, her tea cup poised between tabletop and mouth. She smiled, and it seemed she looked brighter this morning. Not nearly as white and drawn as on previous days. Perhaps the vapors she battled were on their way out.

"Thank you, Oliver. We shall enjoy our day out and be all the livelier this evening for having seen the sights and sounds of our fine city."

## Chapter 17

Lady Gregory was a smart woman. The ride, with warm wind against their cheeks and sunshine upon their parasols, was refreshing. Amy tilted her head back, closed her eyes and slanted her face so a sliver of sunlight touched her cheeks.

"Whatever are you doing? Why, you will be wrinkled before you are wed if you persist showing your skin to the sun. Why, you know better."

Miranda could be so starched she fairly squeaked, so the scolding was not shocking.

Amy did not open her eyes, nor did she move her face, when she answered. "As I have no intention to do that anytime soon, I may as well enjoy myself. And as for knowing better…why, dear sister, I wise enough not to fret away today in anticipation of tomorrow. It will come to no good, engaging in that sort of thinking."

Lord Gregory refused the outing so Oliver sat beside his mother on the seat across from them. He chuckled when Lady Gregory murmured.

But, Miranda was true to form. Like a dog with a bone, she would not surrender.

"Really, how can you say such things? We need to keep our sights on tomorrow. There is no sense squandering your future for a bit of sunshine. It is preposterous."

Oliver cleared his throat. "I am not sure it is not a

fine idea, to feel the warmth of the day upon one's face. It heats the soul, I think. And while I am all for considering the future, enjoying the present is also a rather good endeavor."

All their lives, aside from the incident a few years back when he was indisposed, Oliver had been Lucie's reasonable, older brother. Miranda, the stodgy-before-her-time character. She, the wild one. And Lucie? Well, Lucie had been perfect from the very first breath.

Hearing his reason tempered with a bit of her wild streak brought Amy upright. She swung her head to catch his gaze, intending to smile, but that thought vanished on a sudden wave of nausea.

"Oh!" She clutched her parasol tightly and leaned forward. Closing her eyes, she concentrated on not being ill. But the movement of the barouche, coupled with the abrupt spinning in her head, forced her eyes open instantly. It was better to see her white boot tips than the swirling colors on the backs of her eyelids.

"My dear, you are positively green." Lady Gregory sat forward and put her hand on Amy's shoulder. "Shall I have the driver stop?"

She shook her head, which was a rather bad idea.

Miranda's arm was around her, and she had moved her own parasol to provide a circle of shade. "You must allow the doctor to examine you. This has been going on for weeks."

Again, she shook her head. A moan, very unladylike but better than other events that might still escape her lips.

"It is the backward motion." Lady Gregory stood. The conveyance was large enough to stand comfortably between the seats. "Oliver, help her into my spot. Going backward could make anyone ill."

She allowed him to help her up. Two steps and she crossed the space, doing a minor dance move with her hostess on the center floorboard. Oliver put a steadying hand on her arm, and she lowered herself to the bench. It put her in close proximity to the only man among them, but propriety be damned. It was better to hold the contents of her stomach than refuse to sit beside a man.

They rode in blessed silence for a short while. She felt all gazes upon her but did not look up at anyone until she was sure she was not going to embarrass herself. Finally, she raised her head from her hands.

"Better, my dear?" Lady Gregory's smile was kind, her voice gentle.

"Much." She swallowed. "Thank you."

"Why, we have all had the collywobbles riding backward. These silly things should have two forward-facing seats. Now, that would make more sense."

The man beside her was polite enough that he scooted to the far side, putting space between his body and hers. The seat was wide enough that she did not feel trapped.

"Are you sure you are well enough to continue?" Oliver's tone held concern. "We can turn around right here, if you wish."

She met his gaze, saw mirrored in his eyes what she heard in his voice. "I am fine, thank you."

A slight lift of one eyebrow. "Fine, eh?"

Teasing was better than concern. She must look improved enough that he could raise that brow.

"That's right. I am fine. And I do not wish to turn around. Why, we are nearly halfway there."

Hyde Park in the Season teemed with carriages. It

was a place to see and be seen, the sort of indulgence any woman enjoyed. Of course, they would stay far from Rotten Row, and its speed-seeking set astride horseback. As well, the Ladies' Mile was out of the question, with Oliver insistent that no one be that fully vulnerable. A turn around the Ring, covering the gravel roadway at a sedate pace, was precisely what everyone needed—and what they would get. The drivers of all three carriages were aware of the plan. And, Oliver had apprised the women of his intent as well.

Had she cared to be seen it would have held the promise of excitement, but in her situation the best she could hope for was a pleasant few hours to take her mind from her own troubles.

"As you wish." He did not press, and she was grateful.

Lady Gregory indicated a hedge dripping with red Morning Glories. "Always one of my favorite flowers. Too bad they don't arrange well. I would love to have my maid bring them into my room, but they simply do not stay as lovely cut as they are on the vine."

"They are pretty. And hummingbirds find them very appealing." Miranda supplied the ornithological fact with a nod. "Any red flower, it seems, will attract a hummingbird."

Oliver waited a few moments. "Speaking of maids, I have not seen one of ours around the place in a few days."

His mother raised an eyebrow. Amy kept her amusement to herself; the gesture was almost identical to the one he used so often.

Apple trees make apples, she thought. He was certainly an apple from the Gregory tree.

"Whatever do you mean? We have a number of household staff. It seems odd that you look for one in particular."

"I was not looking." He sounded a tad ruffled. "I am just saying that I have not seen this young woman in a few days, is all. I wondered if she is...ah, well, perhaps she is ill. That is what came to mind."

Mollified, his mother looked to Miranda, then met Amy's gaze. "He always has been considerate, hasn't he? All his life, thinking about others. I should not be surprised he notices a missing maid."

"Yes, well, it is in his nature to be considerate." Amy paused, giving the older woman a smile. "He has been brought up to think of others, thanks to you and Lord Gregory. You have raised him to be a true gentleman."

"Thank you, my dear. We have done our best, although being a parent is never easy." Lady Gregory moved her parasol from one hand to the other. She gave a tiny sniff, then added, "As you will see when the time comes, it is a matter of creating a balance of common sense, discipline and, of course, love. All in the correct measure."

"I will remember that. For when the time comes." She wished she had never broached the topic. It had seemed safe at the outset but had taken an abrupt turn into perilous waters. She steered it back to Oliver, and his missing maid, turning the attention to his original question. "But, the maid...you say you haven't seen the young woman?"

"I have not. And it is my duty to keep track of those in our employ, to be sure they are well cared for and safe. But this young lady seems to have vanished."

His mother clicked her tongue against her teeth. "I doubt anyone has vanished. Why, you make it sound as if Willowbrook is a house full of magicians."

"I did not mean that, Mother."

"Which maid? Perhaps we can put the speculation to an end, if you have a name. Or, even a description, although I do admit many of the younger ones all look the same to me. Starched, proper and fresh."

"Bridget. She is the one I have not seen in days."

"Well, of course, you are right. She may as well have vanished."

Amy watched the man beside her. He leaned forward, elbows on his knees, a pose he favored, and asked, "Mother, what do you mean?"

They were just entering the park. Carriages vied for position on the wide lane. Horses clip-clopped, their paces so sedate those they conveyed hardly felt any movement beneath them. The sounds of laughter, and voices calling to one another. All very happy, and colorful. Women wore brightly patterned dresses and hats, and men twirled walking sticks as they strolled paths between low-hanging willow trees.

"Bridget quit our employ. Very suddenly, I am afraid. No explanation, just sheer insistence that she leave immediately." She waved to someone in a neighboring carriage, the smile on her face giving no hint to the conversation in the barouche. "It is as if she were afraid of something. Or, in trouble. I do not know which, Oliver. But I will say, I miss her flower arrangements in the hallway."

Chapter 18

Bond Street was not altogether sedate after dark. Women were in short supply, unless the Haymarket wares were to be counted. But respectable women were not out on the streets in certain parts of the city after dark. Bond Street and its neighboring alleyways were decidedly off limits.

Will pressed his body tightly into the doorway, making no effort to hide the fact he would rather be snug in his cottage with Vivian than standing across from an opium den. If Oliver had a good, sweet woman waiting for him he wouldn't want to be here, either.

But Oliver didn't have a woman and wished he didn't have to go inside the place again. And Bridget's sudden exit from their household had to mean something. As the one responsible for all things manor related, he was compelled to investigate.

"What is the plan? I assume you *do* have a plan."

Will averted his gaze when a daringly dressed woman walked their way. She attempted to catch their attention, but when one studied his boot tips and the other turned his back on her, she kept walking.

"We shall go in the back door. The kitchen, where we have already been. They won't expect that."

"I am not taking another of those drinks. Vivian was not at all pleased when I came home reeking of cheap alcohol."

Ah, the pleasures of marriage, he mused. One day he might—if he were lucky—know the joy of the union but until then he could only guess.

"You do not need to drink. We just want to speak with that old woman again. Perhaps we can convince her to tell us more about Bridget's visit. It is the key to solving why she was here, and where she has gone."

Will rarely dug his heels in about anything, but the look on his face told a tale. He did not want to go inside. They had been through many scrapes, and Will had never let him down. He'd been there through every moment of the madness that nearly killed him, pulled Oliver from the depths of despair, and nursed him back to health.

He couldn't force the man to do something that so clearly made him uncomfortable. A year ago he never would have attempted to enter a place serving drugs and alcohol on his own, but he was stronger now. There had to be a time when he took a chance and believed himself capable of willpower to withstand temptation. This was the time.

"I will be back in two shakes." He took two steps, put a hand up when Will tried to follow him. "No, really. I am fine. You stay here, keep an eye out for our missing maid. I will nip in the back door, visit Old Dorinda and be back before you even know I'm gone."

"I should accompany you. It is…" A hard shrug. "It is not a good idea for you to go in there at all. Alone? Definitely not one of our best plans."

He hated that his past still haunted him. It was something he was so ashamed of having fallen into that there were moments when he could not stand himself for having been that stupid. But there was no way to alter the past. The most he could do was decide to make the most of the life he had managed to salvage. Pulling oneself up out of a swamp was bound to leave some grime in places no one wanted, but that didn't mean he couldn't feel clean again eventually.

One step in front of the other, Oliver reminded himself. One bad patch did not define a man.

"I can do this." He paused and ran a hand across his cheek. Clean shaven, well-dressed, the kind of man no one would suspect of harboring such a dirty secret. Well, everyone had secrets. "I assure you, it will be fine. I will be fine. And, once I see the potion maker, we can leave."

"I will wait until the clock strikes the quarter-hour, no longer. If you are not out by then, I am going in."

They looked at the large clock face on the building nearby. It was high up but not so high the moonlight didn't illuminate the hands. Twenty minutes was not a lot of time, but it would have to do. He had no doubt his man would do as he said.

"Then I'd best not linger here with you. I will be out, and hopefully with some answers."

He headed across the street. The truth, he did not have a real plan in mind. He did not even know what he hoped to gain by seeing the old woman again. But since it was the only thread linking them to Bridget at this point, pulling it might yield something useful.

Had Nick not been so ill he would have questioned Lucie about her maid's sister. But his own sister had more than enough on her mind, and didn't need to be bothered trying to find out what the maids were doing with mysterious potions procured from dubious establishments.

No, it fell to him to get to the bottom of this.

The alley was deserted. A rat skittered into the darkness near a wall when he walked past, but it was the only sign of life. The air was heavy, reeking of humanity pressed too closely together. Cooking smells, unwashed bodies, urine. None reminded him of their excursion in the park earlier, where flowery scents had threatened to overpower him. Now he wished for the dripping rose hedges and their floral aroma.

Oliver knocked on the kitchen door. Beyond, he heard sounds. Pots being shifted about, a spoon clanking against iron, wood tossed onto a grate. He knocked a second time.

When no one answered his knocking, he lifted the latch and swung the door wide. The room was not bustling the way it had been the other time he had seen it. Now, only a young cook standing over a big pot. If his nose did not deceive him, she stirred beef stew. So ordinary, a meal for a family being prepared in a place where illicit activity and debauchery took place.

She did not turn when he came in, so he kept his footsteps light and moved slowly. No need to attract undue attention. Old Dorinda's quarters lay just beyond the door, to the right, so he stepped closer, holding his breath and praying he would not be found out.

Oliver reached the door, so he lifted the latch and pushed it open, just ever-so slightly. He squeezed into the room, closed the door quietly behind him and turned.

"I knew you would be back." She sat at her work table. Dried clumps of herbs and flowers spread before her. A large knife in one hand, while the other gathered and bundled the herbs. She did not bother to look up, just continued to chop, then push the pieces to the side. A mound of green, mixed with some orange and yellow bits, sat beside the mortar and pestle.

He ventured closer.

"How did you know?"

A low cackle. "Oh, I know things. No one needs to tell Old Dorinda anything. I'm the one who does the telling."

Standing on the other side of her table, he put the question to her. "Do you recall the young maid we inquired about a few days ago?"

She nodded. Kept with her chopping. Still, did not meet his gaze.

"She has gone missing." He hoped the woman had a sympathetic bone in the wizened old body. "I am looking for her."

"Of course you are."

If he wanted information, he would need a more compelling story.

"My sister..."

Without looking up, she asked, "You expect me to believe that young maid is your relation? You, a man who is more likely to give orders to a maid than share parents with one. She is not your blood, sir. I am old, but I am not stupid."

This was not going well. He was not used to people not giving him the answers he sought when he asked questions.

"I did not intend to imply you are stupid. I apologize, ma'am. Please forgive me." He held his arms wide, throwing himself on any merciful impulse she might have. "I am worried about the young woman. I am only trying to locate her to see if she needs help.

She is sibling to my own sister's lady's maid. My mother is upset because the young lady left our employ very hastily. We are concerned, is all. Just very worried."

The explanation was enough to make her put the knife down and look up at him. She didn't say anything for a long moment. Then, a slow nod. "I believe you."

"It is the truth."

"Are you the man who sent that young lady to someone like me?"

He suspected what her potions did for women who were forced to use them. It went unspoken between them, a heavy feeling in the room that neither acknowledged.

"I do not understand." He did not look away when she scrutinized his face. It was a test he was determined to pass.

"You know what she came after. All men know there are places like this for women to get what they need in times when nothing, and no one, else can help. You are a wise man…you are aware of these things." Old Dorinda picked up her knife and gathered a new bunch of dried flowers.

"I am not the one who sent her in search of something to make a—" He could hardly say it, but she was done with him unless he stepped up. "Baby go away."

The old woman had raised the knife in preparation to resume chopping. At his words, she paused, holding it in the air above the flower bundle. One long, deep breath, then a slow exhale.

She looked up at him and shook her head. "That girl didn't come for something to get rid of a baby."

Confusion made him speak without thinking. "What, then? What was she here for?"

"Something to make a baby." The words were spoken so softly, he leaned closer. "That's what she came to me for."

Chapter 19

The manor had never seemed confining before, but it certainly did now. Amy walked from window to window, looked out on the lovely grounds and sighed. Beauty beyond the glass stretched as far as the eye could see, yet it mattered not at all. She barely saw any of it—and did not appreciate the scenery one bit.

A midday rain shower kept everyone indoors. It had stopped sprinkling, but no one was inclined to go out when all was damp and the ground soggy.

Nick and Lucie were still in their rooms although there had been talk of the two perhaps emerging for afternoon tea. It would be the first time since that awful incident, so preparation in the kitchen was in full swing. Lady Gregory wanted something special for the event.

Miranda had been unusually quiet recently. Amy had noticed her dear sister's more pronounced demeanor but really, with a true bluestocking who could tell a blue mood from an introspective one? It wasn't the first time the other had been subdued and it surely would not be the last. For some, a quiet nature was simply part of their personality.

She had always been grateful she was not the quieter sister. Although, had she been, she would never have been in this predicament. Surely her sibling knew better than to do what she had done, and would never have allowed anything untoward to occur.

It was a good thing their parents were abroad. Her ruination would take weeks to reach their ears. By that time, she would have a plan in place. What plan? She had no idea whatsoever, but one had to come to her eventually.

Running a fingertip across the polished window sill, she looked toward the lane leading from the manor toward the cottages. Many of the staff lived in a wing set aside for them. A few very special people, married couples mostly, were given cottages to reside in. Just past the orchard, a short walk through the greenery lining the lane, a homey little village within the manor grounds. No merchants, of course, but a tidy group of homes, each with a stone walkway and flower beds.

Vivian and Will had a cottage. She had never seen it, but her friend spoke about the place often. Suddenly it seemed the only way out of the dark mood that gripped her, an escape to someplace warm and welcoming.

It was poor taste to pop in uninvited and unannounced, but she did not care. Society be damned—she needed to get out before her mind was lost.

She turned, headed down the hallway to her room, and opened the door. Inside the closet, pelisse, bonnet, and umbrella in a dark green that complemented the gown she wore. She dressed in a hurry, mindful that her Abigail could return at any moment with her freshly laundered clothes or polished boots.

She left her room, closed the door behind her and slipped down a side staircase. It was used mostly by the servants, but fortunately none were about, and she made it to a side entrance without detection.

The back terrace was deserted, of course. The stones shining, still wet from the rain, and probably slippery. Amy took care not to fall and bent at the waist to creep beneath the wide windows in Lady Gregory's sitting room. She did the same when she passed Lord Gregory's library.

The edge of the terrace met the lawn at the bottom of a wide stone staircase. That, too, was slick so she held the railing tightly, feeling wetness seep into her white gloves. When her toes hit the bottom, her slippers became damp as they touched the wet lawn.

She did not care about her clothing. All she wanted was to escape—even if the outfit she had on ended up in the rubbish bin by afternoon. Fisting her skirt in her hand, she ran down the lawn toward the lane. Once, she nearly lost her footing to a moss-covered stone, but she righted herself and kept moving toward the point where the lane disappeared into the trees.

****

When Vivian had come to spend the Season at Willowbrook Manor last year, she never dreamed she, the poor relation from Stropshire, would find love and end up living a happily-ever-after life at the grandest place she had ever seen. Her mother and brother, Liam, lived in one of the small cottages as well, and the miracle that brought the change in their fortunes was due in complete measure to the shared, long-lost friendship between Lady Gregory and Vivian's mother.

If that didn't make one believe in miracles, Vivian was sure nothing else could ever accomplish the feat. They were no longer in a cold, drafty apartment, working long hours to put meager food on their table. Life took on a whole new meaning when one was warm and well-fed.

And, when one was loved.

William Fulbright was the kind of man she had always dreamed of but never believed she would meet. He was thoughtful, funny, smart. A good, solid, sensible person, not given to fits of fancy or delusions of having more than a happy, healthy life. They wanted the same things, and since they married her life had been filled with joy.

No more long, hard days laboring over gowns others would wear. While Will was Oliver's assistant, they were as close as brothers. And she was a relation to the duke and duchess, albeit distant, so that gave them a foot up the social ladder. They could have pressed the issue and taken full advantage of the associations but were completely content to spend their time together doing very ordinary things.

Vivian loved keeping her own house. The cottage was small, with two bedrooms, a sitting room, sewing room, kitchen and dining room. A wide hallway separated the living area from the sleeping quarters. And a second story, one large room, would make the perfect playroom for the baby when it was old enough for such things.

Despite the midday rain, sunshine slanted through the wide front window. She sat in a comfortable armchair positioned to catch the sunlight. Her feet were raised on a footstool with an intricately-patterned needlework cover. It was a wedding gift from Lady Gregory. The stitched violets and greenery were beautiful, evidence of a lifetime of embroidery practice. The footstool came in quite handy, especially now when Vivian's ankles were so puffy.

Doctor Fairweather assured her the ankles, as well as her growing midsection, were all perfectly normal and expected consequences of being in her condition. Having been malnourished and slight all her life, accepting her blooming girth was not easy.

When the knock came upon the front door, she thought she imagined it. In the evening, Jemma, the cook who firmly believed any woman getting ready to bear a child should drink ginger and chamomile tea so delivered the concoction like clockwork, might call. Then, the door might feel a visitor's rapping but midday? She must be growing delirious from the damp air.

The second time, she knew it was not her imagination.

She pushed herself to her feet, dropped her sewing onto the chair cushion and went to the door. A wide, heavy wooden door, good for keeping out drafts but requiring a lot of effort to pull open. She tugged hard— so hard, that when it swung inside she stumbled backward two steps.

"Oh, my goodness. Here, let me help you." Amy rushed inside, grabbed her, and held on until her feet were no longer tangled. "Better now?"

"Much, thank you. What a way to welcome you to our home, falling into the hallway so you must rescue me." Vivian ran a hand down the front of her dress, smoothed her skirt, and composed herself. Finding Amy on her doorstep was a surprise. Falling with the door was something she had done many times over.

"The door weighs more than you do."

The visitor stood on the threshold with a smile on her face. It occurred to her that the unexpected guest awaited an invitation, so Vivian swept a hand, motioning her inside.

"Please, come in. It is a lovely surprise to see you."

"Am I intruding?" Amy stood just inside the doorway, glancing around with a blush creeping up her neck. "I really am being so rude and presumptuous to appear here this way. Really, should I go?"

Vivian tugged her friend inside and closed the door with a thump. It latched, shutting the world outside and making it near impossible for her guest to dash back out.

"Certainly not. It is so nice to see you—and such a diversion. It has been so dreadfully quiet; I love it that you have come to visit." She put her arm through the other's and walked into the sitting room. "You have come to visit, haven't you?"

"If you don't mind."

Vivian motioned to the chair opposite hers. Just as they entered, a fresh wave of sunlight infused the space. With the fire crackling in the grate, the room was warm, cozy and cheerful. They sat.

"Not only do I not mind, I am very happy to see you. Would you like some tea?"

"I don't want you to go to any trouble on my account."

Amy's gaze swept the room.

The cottage was comfortable and by far the nicest home she'd ever had, but Vivian was conscious of the fact that to someone like the woman seated across from her, this must seem very humble.

"It is no trouble at all. I was going to make myself a pot of ginger and chamomile tea anyhow. It settles my tummy like nothing else can." When her visitor put a hand over her own stomach, she asked, "And how are you doing with your digestive delicacy? Any better?"

"I do wish I could say it is gone but…it comes. And it goes. And…" A helpless shrug. "It is nasty, feeling so unsettled all the time."

She quite agreed, it was frightfully nasty wondering whether one's stomach would flip or flop without warning. She was at the point where it happened less often, but the memory hadn't faded.

"I will make the big Brown Betty. I have some calming almond biscuits, as well."

Amy removed her pelisse and gloves and laid them across the back of the chair.

"I would like that. I hope I am not intruding, but Vivian I do need to confide in someone."

The earnest tone tugged her heartstrings. They had all wondered what troubled Amy and now, it seemed, she was going to find out. With a prayer for enough wisdom to be of assistance, she nodded.

"We shall visit. And confide. I promise, Amy, to do whatever I can to make you smile again. Why, I very much miss your sunny disposition—and hate seeing you so glum."

"It shows?"

"Oh, you sweet thing. How could it not? You've gone from the cheeriest person we know to someone who carries a weight on her shoulders. It's time to share the weight. You will feel better when you do."

"Yes, I think I will. That is why I came to see you. I truly need to unburden myself. That is, if you are willing to listen."

Vivian's heart swelled. She had not been part of life on the estate for very long, yet she was chosen as a confidante. It was one of the highest honors of her lifetime, to be thought of so well.

"I am. But not until we have a pot and biscuits between us. Relax, my dear. I shall be right back."

Chapter 20

Keeping the peace on an estate was typically a simple affair. The Lord of the manor dictated what rules he believed should be kept on his property, then hired men to ensure those who worked for him adhered to those guidelines. Very clean, with no gray area. Those few who did not toe the line were dismissed. Those who behaved accordingly stayed on and were afforded the means to properly care for themselves as well as their families. The system had been working for generations and would continue to work the same way for generations to come. It was a way of life. And, it was one that worked for everyone involved.

Once beyond the borders of an estate, however, things changed. Lawless behavior often created chaos, a reason so many carriages of footmen accompanied the lords and ladies of the realm. Seeking justice and retribution were hit and miss prospects. Mostly, crimes went unpunished. The wicked preyed on the moneyed and were rewarded when they went on their way without repercussions.

Oliver and Will had been to Town yet again to see the solicitor. The aged gentleman worked with the local law enforcement to discover where the two men who escaped had gone, but there was no success in the matter. The man with the broken leg was recovering in the stable boy's cabin. He had given the other two up and once his situation had been uncovered, Oliver offered the man employment. When his leg healed, he would work for his dinner rather than steal for it. And he would be able to care for his family. To that end, it had been arranged that the kitchen would deliver food to the thief's family so they did not starve while the man was laid low.

Willowbrook Manor and its owners lifted those around them. They would never be one of the wealthy set who oppressed others in order to rise higher in the world. It was not Gregory tradition to do so, and Oliver prayed it would never become so.

He and Will rode home in near silence. There was little to say on the matter.

And there was a point where a man had to admit defeat, whatever the situation. It was clear that those who nearly killed Nick were long gone. Their families, impoverished and frightened, swore they knew not of the pair's whereabouts. They, too, had been fed, beneficiaries of the Gregory generosity.

The chapter was closed. Thankfully, Nick looked as if he were going to survive the ordeal. So at least that was something to be glad about.

Other than that, they needed to take greater precautions. During the Season, when women wore expensive finery and precious heirloom jewels, the carriages they rode were more inclined to attract thieves. From this point on, he would not allow a carriage to convey anyone without an escort carriage of footmen. Having anyone hurt was not going to happen again.

Will finally broke the silence. "I am glad it finally stopped raining. And the sun is peeking out from behind the clouds. That is a good sign, I think."

"Yes, it is. We all hate gloomy days. There are enough of them during the winter months that we need not bear them during these warm days."

Their horses' hooves beat a steady cadence against the firmly packed road. They were nearly where the carriage had been come upon. No trace remained, but everyone knew the spot where the incident had taken place.

Oliver shook his head. "It seems wrong that some may cause bodily harm to others, yet earn no punishment for the misdeed. I know there are many things that are not especially fair or good. Still, it does not make the truth any less difficult to fathom."

He was not with unrealistic goals or lofty ideals. He had seen the seamy side of life. Hell, he had been part of it, even. But that did not make him unaffected to injustice when he saw it. And when it impacted a member of his family it burned a hole in his gut.

"I believe people get what they deserve. Look, we may not see justice done for Nick and Lucie, but that does not mean it will not be served. It may not be in the manner to which we are accustomed, or in a way that makes us comfortable, but I do believe that eventually the two unrepentant, cowardly thieves will get their due."

Will reached down and smoothed a hand over his mount's glossy mane. The horse was his favorite, a big bay purchased last Season. It was the horse that caused Oliver and Vivian to argue—heatedly—and admit that neither felt the other a suitable match, despite what their mothers wished for them.

He had to acquiesce. Will's logic was indisputable.

Even in personal relationships, people got what they deserved. Look at how he and Vivian had not made a good match at all, yet Will and Vivian…well, they deserved each other. They were so mutually suitable and made each other so blissful that it explained why he and she were like oil and water.

"Yes, you are probably right. I am just not dealing well with having to break the news that no one seems confident the two scoundrels will ever be brought up on charges for what they did. My sister is going to be upset."

"How can you be sure? She may not give a fig about those men. Why, having her husband alive is probably all she cares about."

They turned in at the entrance to the manor. Two uniformed men stood sentry and bowed when they passed.

He still hadn't told Will the true nature of Old Dorinda's confession. The time had never come, not even when he emerged from the manse on Bond Street. By then, it was just beginning to rain and they had to rush back to the townhouse before becoming drenched. Little time for conversation since, which was fine with Oliver. He did not know what to make of the old potion maker's statement. He knew very little about women's affairs of the body as even less about the workings of their hearts. And to discuss such a private matter—even with Will—seemed too much.

"I hope that is the case. I hate to see her upset. And, since I have been the subject of her unhappiness in the past, I have no wish to disappoint Lucie again. Ever."

\*\*\*\*

The scene in the parlor was a pleasant one. Lord and Lady Gregory sat beside the hearth, tea cups in hands and smiles on their wrinkled faces. They never looked happier than when surrounded by those they loved.

Nick lay propped on a chaise, his bad leg atop a mound of pillows and a blanket covering him nearly from chest to toes. Lucie sat beside him, in a chair near his head. It was clear she shielded him. From what, Oliver wasn't sure, but he saw the protective set to her chin and recognized it.

"Well, isn't this the ideal afternoon tea party?" Oliver went to kiss his mother's cheek. Her skin was still soft and she smelled of roses. He touched his lips to her face, then straightened and turned to his father. "You all sound so cheerful, it does a man's heart good to hear the laughter."

Lord Gregory waved a pipe in one hand. It was, per doctor's orders, unlit.

"It does do a man's heart good. Now, if I could just get Fairweather to agree that a pipe is just as beneficial, I might be the happiest man this side of London." He scowled at the unlit meerschaum. It was a family heirloom, but if Father did not loosen his grip on the old carved piece it might not survive for future generations.

Oliver did not care whether the pipe survived or not. He did not partake in any activity that might be habit-forming. Pipe smoking, if Father were to be believed, was definitely a habit-forming endeavor.

Let the pipe be crushed like so much powder, he thought.

Mother put down her cup on the cherry wood table beside her chair. She furrowed her brow and waved a hand toward her husband.

"Be content with renewed health. Nothing else, not even that silly old pipe, can be so imperative you would put your well-being in jeopardy." She turned and gave an impatient shake of her head. "Really, your father can be difficult when he chooses to be. That pipe…"

"We all have that talent, I'm afraid." He stood beside the fire and looked around. His parents. Nick and Lucie, so wrapped up in their own merrymaking they hadn't noticed anyone else. Miranda, her nose in a book, sat on the window seat. It was odd she did not attempt to catch his eye, but it was also a relief. No need to feel like a small gray mouse beneath the stare of a hungry cat, which was often the case when they were together.

Will followed him in and had given his best to everyone in a general sort of way. Now, he stood in the center of the room, a puzzled look pulling his features tight.

Oliver realized what the man searched for. Or, more precisely, who he hoped to see. "Where is Vivian, Mother?"

Lady Gregory looked between Oliver and Will. "I have no idea. She has not been here all day. I admit, I am somewhat worried. A woman in her condition… well, perhaps she is just resting."

His mother turned to face Will. "Won't you please persuade her to take a maid? Or a cook? Really, it would put my mind at rest if I knew she wasn't carrying the household burdens. She is a relation, you know, so there is nothing amiss with a small staff. Please, talk with her about it."

Will was in a tight spot, caught between servant

and family. "I will speak with her, I promise." Oliver caught his gaze. "But first, I must find her. If you will all excuse me."

"I will go with you." He kissed his mother's cheek, waved to Miranda who still hadn't looked up at him and said to the lovebirds in the corner, "It is good to see you two up and about. We shall visit later, if you are up to it."

"No guarantees." Nick held Lucie's hand, and traced a languid thumb across the smooth skin in a way that was so intimate Oliver looked away. "We might be forced to, ah, retire early. It is, as one would guess, a strain to remain in such a position."

Lucie's giggle warmed his heart. She and Nick married out of duty but loved purely for the wonder and beauty of it. Theirs was a blessed union, and he was immensely grateful it hadn't been cut short.

"Well, then we will visit when we are able. It is very good to see you looking well." He winked at Lucie. "Do not tire the man out, little sister. He needs his rest, you know."

"Oliver!" She arranged her lovely features into a scandalized expression but could not hold it for long. Covering her mouth with her free hand, she laughed.

True music to everyone's ears, to hear Lucie so giddy.

Chapter 21

On the terrace, Oliver turned to Will. "Amy is not inside, either. Wherever can they be? Do you think they are together?"

Will raked his fingers through his hair. It was the first time since Vivian came to Willowbrook Manor that she hadn't presented herself in the sitting room for an afternoon with the other women. When they had other plans, or were away from the manor, of course was different, but this was a perfectly average day and as such should have found her in the room with the rest of the family.

"I hardly know. This is the first time she has not been inside of an afternoon. Even when she felt so dastardly, just two or three weeks past, she managed to get herself together to spend sitting room time. It is unsettling that she is not in there."

Oliver's gut clenched. The highway robbery was still fresh in his mind.

"And Amy. It is not like her to miss the opportunity to socialize." She loved spinning small gossipy tales, sharing news of Town, comparing dance steps and embroidery stitches too much with the other women to miss the chance to do so. Something was amiss—he felt it.

"Where would they be?" Will glanced around the wide space before them, but there was no sign of either woman. "The rose garden?"

"It is as good a place as any to search. I found Amy there not long ago. Perhaps she is painting again."

"But Vivian does not paint." Will turned and put a hand on the latch on the door they had just passed through. "But she does enjoy speaking with the Abigail who does most of the minor needlework here. Perhaps she is with her, in that bright sewing room on the third floor."

"You look there, and I will dash over to the rose gardens. We will find them. Ask the maid if she has any idea where they might be." Oliver took two steps away from the manor, heading toward the stone steps on the distant side of the terrace. He stopped, turned, and smiled, hoping to ease his friend's concern. "Sometimes I believe the maids know more about us than we know about ourselves."

"Spot on, that." Will opened, then closed the door. Oliver had only gone one more step when Will asked, "By the way, we still haven't discussed what you learned—or didn't learn—about Bridget. Remember, the maid whose predilection for Bond Street left my clothing stinky and my wife wondering where I had acquired eau de spirits?"

His smile was bigger and reached his eyes now that Will had lightened the mood. It was like him to say something jokingly at a time when levity was most needed. The man had a clever streak so wide that had he been a peer he undoubtedly would have made headlines in *The Daily Gazette*.

He did not wish to lie, but he did not wish to divulge the entirety of what he'd learned from Old Dorinda, so Oliver took a middle stance.

"It was as we thought. Bridget went to the potioness for something to deal with...ah, to take care of a female ailment. Nothing new learned from the visit, I'm afraid."

"Well, at least we didn't get soaked by the libations served there. But it does not get us any closer to unraveling the mystery of why the maid has gone, does it? Although..."

Will snapped his fingers.

"Although what?"

"Well, if she *is* in trouble, of the female sort, it does make sense that she might go away." He did not hide the fact that it saddened him to think of the girl in such a plight. "It is unfortunate, but it does happen, Oliver."

Yes, he knew that. Even in the highest points of society, things happened. People were, after all, people. And human desire...sometimes it brought the most well-meaning individual to shame.

But Will did not know the truth. Bridget was less likely to be in that sort of predicament than nearly anyone. If a woman needed to procure something to make a baby, it was very unlikely she was already with child. No, it had to be something else.

Nonetheless, he nodded. "You are probably right. That is it, she has left for a personal female reason. Now, I'm going to check the rose gardens. Hopefully I will find the women there."

"And I will go look in the upstairs sewing room. I know I shouldn't fret so, but Vivian is carrying my child, and even if she weren't, I would worry about her." He sighed, and added, "I suppose this is what it means to be in love."

"I suppose it is."

Oliver walked away, feeling something in his own heart he had never felt before. Amy was not his wife, and she certainly did not carry his child, but he was very concerned about her well-being. Her going missing when he had hoped to spend some time near her, and hear her sweet laugh, tore a hole in the heart he'd believed immune to any woman's influence.

Two hours later, there was still no sign of Amy. He had checked the rose gardens—all three of them—thoroughly. He searched the kitchen gardens, and the old greenhouse his sister favored so much, but they were all empty.

A Folly designed by his grandfather was a short walk from the manor house, but he made the trip. It was a gorgeous place, intricately carved of imported marble, designed for sheer beauty and pleasure. It had been a favorite of his father when he was a boy as well as he and Lucie when they were children, so it was a likely place to find Amy. Beauty attracts beauty, and it seemed she should be there. But he walked the perimeter of the circular building and she was not, as he'd hoped, lingering on one of the wide marble benches set against its outer walls. There was little chance she would have gone inside, but he'd taken the key from its hiding spot behind a carved cherub's figure, inserted it into the heavy lock and pushed the door wide. The inside was, as he feared, empty.

So many horrible scenes ran through his head that he forced himself to disregard them. Before the incident with the carriage being held up, nothing threatening ever happened at the manor. Or, on their neighbors' estates. It was not like the seedier parts of the city; these were pure gentrified properties owned by dukes and earls. The occasional baron might winter outside Town, but there were no unfortunate elements to disrupt their happy lives.

Even the servants were well-behaved. Their situations rarely gave them cause for disquiet, they were all so well kept.

Still, images of Amy set upon by bandits, taken from one of the gardens or lying hurt in a desolate area of the estate tortured him. Oliver did not know when he had come to care so much for the woman. He only knew that he did.

Botheration! Where on earth can she be?

He locked the Folly, secreted the key behind the cherub and took off at a run. Perhaps Will had located his wife by now. If he were lucky, she would know where Amy had gone. And if she did not know, he was going to send the groundskeepers, grooms, and other men—including the household staff, if necessary—searching for her. It would not be tolerated, losing a guest of the manor. Not now, not ever, would it be acceptable for someone to simply disappear.

Chapter 22

Amy cringed. Even the knock on the door sounded angry. "That will be Oliver." Will looked from wife to friend, then shrugged. "If I do not open the door, I suspect he will knock it in."

"Let him in, dear." Vivian sat beside her on the small settee and now patted her hand. "We shall talk some more, but I think now we are ready to face the rest of this lovely day, aren't we?"

They had been that way for hours, holding hands and sharing confidences. Well, Amy had shared mostly, both confessions and a multitude of tears. She had not gotten any harsh judgment from Vivian, only soothing words of encouragement and many back rubs. It had been just what she needed most, a caring ear to listen and other shoulders to help carry the burden of her secret.

She scrubbed her palms over her cheeks, praying the evidence of her tears had not turned her ugly. A Friday-faced female never garnered a man's good attentions, and she did not wish to be seen in such an unflattering light.

"Yes, I do believe we are." When Will turned and went to the door, she reached out and pulled Vivian into a quick embrace. Whispering into the other woman's ear, she said, "Thank you. I feel ever so much better now."

They separated, and arranged their skirts in identical pools of favorable cascades. They put their hands upon their laps, brought smiles to their faces and attempted to appear as carefree as two larks on the sweetest branch of an apple-blossom laden tree.

"I am glad. It is what we are here for, to hold each other up when necessary." She lowered her voice, so only Amy could hear. "Or, as we are about to see, to dress each other down. If that banging on the door and the loud voices at the threshold mean anything, my cousin will not be as easily pacified as my husband was."

She could not have been more correct.

Oliver strode into the room looking every inch the put-upon duke. He looked from Amy to Vivian, then back to Amy again. His eyes flashed, and he made no effort to conceal his annoyance.

Ever the good hostess, Vivian smiled at the second intrusion to her day.

"What a charming surprise—so nice of you to visit us. Finally—you know good and well I have asked you to come by and chat on more than one occasion. I do wish you had let me know you were coming, though. I would have baked you something special."

He could not treat her badly, it was not something he had been born to do, so he bowed, first to Vivian, then to Amy. They inclined their heads, kept their seats and smiled.

When he spoke, he was somewhat out of breath.

"I did not plan to arrive unannounced." He paused, inhaled deeply, scowling a bit. Even winded and agitated, he cut a handsome form. "I have been searching for you two ladies. It was, ah, disconcerting when neither of you appeared this afternoon with the others."

Amy was glad for this time with which to compose herself. She wasn't sure her voice would not betray the fact she had been sobbing when Will appeared. He seemed inclined to keep her secret. For now. But, it might not take much for Oliver to guess the nature of her time in the cottage had not been entirely without duress. And that just would not do at all. So, she kept quiet.

Fortunately, the other woman did not need her to keep the conversation cordial.

"My goodness, but you sound breathless. Are you well?" Vivian put a hand on her midsection, as if discomfited by the realization. Instantly both men lost their fierce looks.

Will went to stand beside his wife and placed a hand on her shoulder. "You should not worry yourself about any of us. Of course he is well, my dear. Aren't you?"

Oliver nodded. "Yes, yes, I am fine. I am, I admit, somewhat breathless, but there is a good explanation for that. I have been running, although I am loathe to admit it. I feel rather foolish just now. I…"

Oliver's gaze met hers, and it was as if the others were not present for several long moments. He glanced down to her slippers, which peeked out from beneath her gown. Then, up to her face again. He lingered, looking into her eyes with questions she could not acknowledge.

If he guessed she had been crying there was nothing she could do about that. But, he would never uncover the secrets shared this day in this very room.

That much she knew.

"I was concerned about you ladies." Oliver took a deep breath, then smiled. He did not look completely appeased, but he was swiftly losing his agitation. "I could not find either of you and worried something might have befallen you. I apologize if I presented myself badly just now. I have no excuse save the truth." He met her gaze and held it. "I was concerned."

She could have fallen into his eyes, they were so dark and welcoming. She had no right to feel anything for the man, but she did. It was different—far different—from how she felt about Lyle Roarke and that was a very good thing. Whatever she and Lyle had had—because it was definitely over between them—had led to heartache and that was something she did not wish to ever again feel, not for any man.

"We were right here all the time," Vivian said smoothly. "Weren't we?"

Amy nodded. "Yes, we have had a pleasant afternoon. This cottage is so homey and comfortable, and Vivian has been kind enough to share the serenity with me."

"It has been a wonderful way to spend the afternoon." Vivian took her hand and clasped it tightly in her own. She smiled so gaily no one would ever believe there had been sobbing in this very spot just an hour prior. "We need to do this again, very soon. You brought a distraction that I so desperately needed. Thank you, Amy, for visiting today."

She played along, flashing a bright smile. "We do need to repeat this, and soon. But now, I should be getting back. Why, if Oliver wondered where we were, my sister should also be speculating." She stood, eyeing her pelisse and bonnet where they lay on the chair across the room. To get to them, she had to pass close to Oliver.

"I will walk you back," he said, stepping aside to let her pass.

The words made something inside her skip, but for the first time in weeks it was not a sign her stomach was about to rebel. No, this little hop in her belly was pleasant, so she gave him an acknowledging smile. "I would like that very much, thank you."

Chapter 23

The sun hung low in the sky when they began the stroll back to the manor. Oliver did not rush, instead pacing his steps so that she had to slow to match his stride. He did not want this time with Amy to end too quickly.

She seemed content to meander, and fell into step beside him. It was funny, they had known each other for ages, had grown up together and even partnered during dances, but none of that felt as intimate as this leisurely walk through the whispering poplars did now. Sunlight dotted the cobblestones at their feet, sending slivers of light along the mossy stones and touching the hemline of the silky gown she wore. He watched, temporarily mesmerized by the motion and light, by the serenity given so freely in the quiet moment.

Scraped knees and a fall from a horse when she was barely a teen had shown him her tears. Some women were red-faced and distressing to watch when they cried. Amy had never been that way. He had never seen her sob or wail, the way some were inclined to do. Instead of making her appearance unfortunate, a tear sliding down her creamy cheek had always infused him with the desire to protect her and wipe the moisture away. He had never done so, of course. It would be highly improper, even with the closeness they shared between their families. But he had still wondered how it might feel to slide a fingertip along her skin, to remove all traces of sadness and soothe her troubled soul.

That had been a fanciful boy's dream. They were no longer children, and souls could not be soothed so simply.

A safe topic, to get the conversation rolling, was called for. But what could he say? He'd stormed into the cottage like an enraged bull. He saw she had shared a confidence and tears with Vivian. And now, he could comment on neither of those. They were too indelicate to be brought up, even though they were probably on her mind as well as his own.

He cleared his throat. "The weather...it is an awfully nice day, isn't it?"

She looked positively relieved.

"Yes, it is lovely. I am so glad the rain stopped early enough to give us time outdoors."

"Better than having one of those all-day rains, isn't it?"

"So much better." When she smiled, the sun dimmed by comparison.

She worried her lower lip, a long-standing childhood habit that had not been outgrown. He was rather glad it hadn't been; watching her, waiting for her next comment, completely engaged his attention.

"I...I, ah..."

"What is it, Amy? Please, tell me what is on your mind." He put his arms behind his back, clasping one wrist with the other hand. It was a pose he favored when thinking, and came naturally as he watched her weigh her next words. It was clear it took effort to consider her thoughts, then give them voice.

He wished she did not find it so difficult to speak

with him. After all, they were friends for so many years. Shouldn't long-standing friends be less studied in their associations?

Amy took a deep breath and let it out on a sigh.

"I just do not feel like going indoors yet. It is such a pleasant afternoon; I just can't bear to be closed inside like a butterfly trapped in its cocoon." She turned to him with wide eyes, and he noticed the golden flecks in her green irises. Enchanting, just like the smile she favored him with. "Would you mind terribly if we take a stroll around the grounds? I would love it if you would consent."

It amused him that she had managed to nearly read his mind. He had been wondering how to broach the same topic, but she had bested him. "It would be my pleasure. But I believe I should be the one asking you to accompany me around the grounds. It is, after all, a venture that would please me more than I can say. I fear I have let you down, not enquiring before you asked. I am, I must admit, supremely chagrined."

"We should not stand on such formality. We have known each other almost since I was in leading strings." She swung her parasol from its satin ribbon, a girlish gesture that caught his attention as fully as her eyes had only moments earlier. He was just seeing how rather amusing women could be. "And I am much too forward by far, asking you to walk with me. Why, if your mother knew, she would shake her head and quite possibly give me a serious talking to in her private sitting room."

It did not go unnoticed that she said his mother, and not her own. His heart dropped as it hit him that had it not been for his own mother, the two sisters would have been completely adrift. And Lucie, as well. Her influence certainly had a stabilizing impact.

Now he began to see why Miranda tried to latch on to him. She had to be pining for a solid male figure in her life. And Amy's silliness? That probably covered the sadness she must feel over not having a typical home.

He realized she waited for his reply, so he pushed aside the images of two parentless girls and managed to pull his features into place. No frown, but a smile. And where there might be tears—had he been the crying type, which he wasn't—a note of cheerfulness to his voice.

"Why don't we just forget how we came to the decision to walk in the sunshine? We shall simply enjoy the walk. That way, I do not need to feel I did not act the gentleman and ask you for the pleasure in a timely fashion. And you, well, you won't need to give a thought to Mother taking you aside to speak with you about a woman's role in a relationship."

Her right eyebrow lifted so high it disappeared beneath an artfully arranged curl where it lay on her forehead. "Ah, so is that it? A 'relationship' is what this is? Why, who can ever tell about these things?"

Her tone left no room to wonder; she teased him, and the smile that accompanied her words lifted his heart higher than it had been in…well, higher than it ever had been, he supposed. Warmth, not from the sun but her presence, suffused him and made his step lighter.

"I did not mean to presume." He tipped his head, lowering his chin toward his chest. "Forgive me, my mouth is not always in step with my brain."

"It is fine. I no longer take what a man says in earnest." Amy put a hand over her lips and looked up at him in shock. She spoke, as he had, without considering her words.

Even when the mouth does not consult the brain, it speaks from the heart.

Allowing her to turn any pinker than she already had would be cruel so he laughed and tugged her hand from her face. Her cheeks were crimson, her eyes round and beautiful, and her lips were open a scant half-inch.

Laughter died on his own lips as desire raced through him. He was, after all, only a man. A man who had just learned how intoxicating a woman's gaze could be, how a captivating giggle affected a heart, how lovely the scent of lavender felt when pulled deeply into the lungs...

He did the unthinkable.

The kiss was oh, so brief, but it sent Oliver's heart hammering in his chest. Desire washed over him, but he controlled himself, tasting her mouth with his and pulling back before she could push him away. She tasted like honey, and cinnamon, and—damn it all, but she tasted like the sun, moon and stars, and he knew it did not make a bit of sense, but that did not matter.

Her breath caught when he released her lips. They stood so close he saw the pulse beat in her temple. Instinct urged him to kiss the spot, but for once his brain spoke up, and he refrained.

"Amy, I..."

He what? What could he say?

He should apologize, but that would be a lie. He wasn't sorry he had kissed her. If anything, he was sorry he hadn't been free to do more than kiss.

She hitched a breath, but did not take a step back. And, she did not slap his face. She just stared, her gaze a mirror of the surprise that overcame him as well.

Oliver swallowed. They were just past the cobblestone lane, out onto the grassy lawn. They were not far from the manor, and if anyone had been on the terrace their indiscretion would surely be noticed. It was unlikely, but possible.

Good manners dictated he step away, so he did. But the moment there was extra space between them, he wished it were not so. The scent of lavender lingered in his head, but the truth was he liked being closer to her than was entirely proper.

"I did not intend to do that." He raked a hand through his hair. Words failed him, so he struggled for something to say. Something proper and placating, because surely she must be upset by his bad behavior. After all, she was a well-bred young woman and not accustomed to men kissing her at will. "I wish I could say I am sorry, but I am not. I cannot lie to you…"

He saw in her gaze what he felt inside. At least, that is how it appeared to his untrained eyes. She looked away, but he carried the vision of her glowing loveliness close to his heart.

She straightened the lower edge of her pelisse although it did not need attention. Then, she pressed her fingers tightly into her gloves, giving each hand a tug to be sure they were where they ought to be. Finally, she laced her fingers together, the parasol dangling from one wrist, and held them before her waist.

It was, he saw, a self-composing moment.

Good she took it, because he was in dire need of one as well.

Suddenly, her sunny disposition vanished, the gleam in her eyes gone. A veil dropped, so opaque her true feelings were nowhere to be seen.

Her voice, so warm a short time ago, was controlled and—he hated to admit it—cold.

"It is fine. I have learned not to believe whatever men say, anyhow. They do as they wish, and we are left to pick up the pieces. If you will excuse me, I find I am not much in the mood for perambulating." He opened his mouth and would have spoken, but she held up a hand. "No, thank you anyhow, but I do not need an escort back to the manor."

"But I—"

"I do not need any help, Oliver. Good day."

He watched helplessly as she turned and walked away from him. She crossed the lawn, her spine stiff and her steps measured, every inch the lady. But he had somehow—completely unwittingly—harmed what had been growing between them. He had no idea what he had done—for she truly seemed to enjoy the kiss—but somehow he would have to make it up to her.

Because if he had his way—and he usually did—he planned to kiss that woman again. And again. And, even, again.

Chapter 24

Lucie ran a hand over her midsection. Flat. Even with the elaborate gown she had donned in celebration of their first dinner downstairs since the robbery, she was svelte. Too svelte for her liking.

Jealousy wasn't an emotion she favored, but the truth was, she was jealous of Vivian's growing shape. Her cousin positively glowed, and the brightest smiles on her face accentuated the bloom of her cheeks. A baby, and so quickly, for the couple. It was a blessing, but Lucie could not help herself—she wished to be blessed in the same exact manner as the fates had seen fit to bestow upon the other woman.

Why, to be raising children so closely matched in ages would be enchanting. If only it could be so, but, as she knew all too well, this was not the month for such optimism. They had failed miserably—yet again—but at least now Nick knew how she felt about his staying near enough to make their family grow.

She had not meant for his confinement, which made it utterly impossible for him to travel. When they discussed her feelings, she asked only that he travel less and stay nearer her more. Not only for the sake of the family they hoped to have, but for them, as well. Nick had gone from stranger who proposed a marriage in name only to her closest companion. He was her confidante. Her teacher on traveling the world. A man who talked as glibly about fashion—what appealed to him, at any rate—as he did about fox hunting. Which, although she listened to his fox tales, she found distasteful.

It did not matter. Friends shared all manner of things. For her husband, it meant discussing fichus and dance slippers. Lucie endured musings on horseflesh, hunting escapades and how to best handle a curricle in wet weather. So, they grew together, and all she asked was he remain near enough that their association had the chance to become even cozier than it already was.

They had been married for just under two years, but it felt as if they had been together forever. She did not remember a time when they were not husband and wife, although she did recall with fondness their first meeting. And, their first dance.

Nick's voice warmed her from the inside out and chased away the collywobbles about her figure. Just a word from the man made her feel there wasn't a single thing wrong in the world.

"You are a vision in that gown, my dear. You shall make the centerpieces wilt, they will be so jealous of your beauty."

She turned to face him. When he'd been injured, the doctor ordered a push chair. It was a handsome conveyance made of warm oak with a carved backrest and padded seat. His bad leg was held up by a wooden leg rest, and if he were to be believed, it was actually a rather comfortable way to move about.

His valet had been incredibly gentle and compassionate, taking pride in not making the rigors of dressing and undressing any more tiring on his lordship than necessary. He'd turned the duke out in fine form tonight, so she nodded and flashed a bright smile.

"Why, you could catch a whole den of bears, you have so much honey dripping from those words. I appreciate your sentiment, but I am quite sure the flowers will be safe." She crossed the sitting room and stood in front of his chair. Leaning down, she adjusted his collar. Then she looked up at the man standing behind the chair and nodded. "Thank you, Randolph. You and his lordship have put his eveningwear to good use. I will bring my husband to the stairs. We shall be there shortly."

"Thank you, your Ladyship. And I shall be waiting at the head of the stairs whenever you are ready to go to dinner."

Randolph was in his early twenties, a strong man who had not had one ounce of trouble caring for an infirmed duke. He lifted her husband, who was not fat but very well-muscled and therefore somewhat heavier than a slighter man would be, without any effort at all. The situation was improving daily, and the man's help made it all less troublesome by far.

When the valet left, closing the door quietly behind him, Lucie gathered her skirt and sat on her husband's lap. He pulled her into his embrace and settled her against his chest. She lay back against him, finding the spot where her head could hear his heart as she tucked her cheek against his shoulder.

"How do you feel, my love? Are you sure you want to go back downstairs?"

"I am fine. Getting stronger every day, and yes, I do want to go down for dinner. We need to take part in family life again. We cannot remain locked up here forever."

She sighed. "Why not? I like being locked in with you."

Nick ran a hand down her arm, his skin warm against hers above the elbow-high white gloves and below the edge of the gown's tulip sleeve. She shivered against him, gooseflesh rising on her in response to his caress.

"Are you cold? Shall we fetch a shawl before we go down?"

He was never inconsiderate. Given the condition of his leg, shoulder and some internal organs, which the doctor refused to discuss, saying only they would heal in their own good time and as long as Nick continued to exhibit normal bodily functions they would not trouble themselves over the damage, had he taken this one opportunity to think only of himself no one would have thought poorly of the man. But he did not, staying true to character even in his battered state.

"I am fine." She turned her head, placed her lips against his jaw and kissed him. The point where a vein beat just below his freshly shaven skin was particularly appealing, so she nuzzled him for a moment, spreading tiny kisses to a place she knew from experience was exceedingly sensitive.

"Mmm…" The rumble made his chest vibrate, so she lifted her face and stared into his eyes. The man was the answer to every dream she had ever had, and even if they lived to be a hundred, there would not be enough days in their lifetimes to satisfy her desire to lock gazes with him.

"Yes?" The question was a whisper, a gentle sound borne on the slightest breath.

"Yes." He put a hand on the back of her neck and

brought her mouth to his. Their kiss, so tender and loving, sent the rest of the world into oblivion. There was nothing, and no one, outside the love they shared. He broke their bond and growled against her neck, "Maybe we should stay up here after all."

The doctor had been clear about refraining from marital activity until Nick was more fully recovered, so she pushed him very gently away.

"I don't think that is a good idea at all." She licked her lips, and smoothed her skirt. She tasted him on her skin, and felt her heart melt. There were times it still amazed her that such a wonderful man was actually her husband. Better yet, he loved her.

"It is a grand idea." He cupped one of her breasts with his free hand, running his fingers across the stiff peak pressed against the shimmery bodice. The gown was made of the sheerest yellow chiffon. So soft and elegant, yet somehow understated. Now, she wondered if her breasts might dent the expensive fabric, her nipples were so hard.

"Doctor Fairweather says—"

He cut her off with a kiss as he wiggled one fingertip over the edge of her bodice and into her gown. His touch against her sensitive areola made her gasp— but he did not stop. And, she did not pull away.

"Doctor Fairweather does not know what he's talking about."

"He is the doctor." She kissed Nick's brow.

His fingers left her breast and found her hand. He pulled it toward his trousers, placing it so the evidence of his desire throbbed hotly against her palm.

Her husband met her gaze with a wicked little grin as he pressed her hand hard against him.

"The doctor does not know how well I am doing." A groan, so deep and throaty it sent chills of desire up Lucie's spine. He took his hand away, yet she continued to caress him. It would have to stop, she knew that, but a few seconds of pleasure were glorious.

"I am glad you are recovering so nicely." She gave him a tiny squeeze as she grinned. "But I am quite sure this type of activity is off-limits for a while. I don't even have to ask the doctor to know that is so."

"But it has been so long, and I miss you." When she took the hand from him, he caught it and brought her fingertips to his mouth. He kissed each one in turn, looking at her as he did so. His lovemaking skills, even out of the bedroom, left her breathless. "It has been too long. A man could go crazy from wanting his wife so much."

She sighed at the pleading in his eyes. Such a schoolboy look, almost impossible to refuse, on such an adult subject. He was right, it had been a long time since they had been close.

"Soon, Nick. We cannot jeopardize your health to satisfy our wanton ways." A giggle when he pulled a face.

"It has been so long I will probably not remember how to be wanton, my dear. Why, the last time we were—"

He stopped short as clarity struck them both dumb.

They last time they had been intimate was the night of the robbery, just minutes before their world turned upside down and they nearly lost each other for good.

Lucie would never forget that day. Never.

And, by the ashen color in Nick's handsome face, neither would he.

Chapter 25

Oliver watched the doorway leading to the front hall, but Amy did not present herself in the parlor with the rest of those in residence so she was not with them when they headed to the dining room. He wished it were possible to just go upstairs, knock on her door and ask her to join them. It was, of course, completely out of the question, but that did not make him any less eager to do so.

It was good that Mother had eased her anxiety over social protocol because with Amy, they would have been only nine at the table. Not ten, but an odd number, something that would have put the hostess at sixes and sevens just a few years back. It was funny what a change of perspective brought on by a series of life-altering experiences could do for a person. He glanced over as she spoke quietly to one of the dining room maids. By the time they were in the room, the extra place setting had been taken away, and the ones nearest moved ever-so slightly to conceal its absence.

The room was set more for family than entertaining. The long, polished table was hidden beneath a starched ivory cloth, white china with hand-painted floral details, silver flatware and sparkling glasses made the prospect of eating pleasurable. It could accommodate many more, but the extra leaves were not in so the maximum number of comfortable diners was an even dozen; with less it there was plenty of elbow room.

Father took his place at the head, and Mother sat to his right. With Nick in the push chair, it was a sensible move to allow him the spot at the far end of the table. Lucie sat beside her husband, on his right. Vivian and Will sat on that side as well, so the remaining chairs were left to him and Miranda.

He waited until she was seated before he took his place beside her. When their napkins had been unfolded and were in their laps, he turned his attention on his dinner partner.

And, chose an unfortunate opening.

"Have you an idea where Amy is? I rather thought to see her at dinner."

He couldn't have stuck his foot any farther into his mouth if he'd tried. There was no way to recall his words although he would have given his favorite horse if it had been possible. The glare Miranda shot him— before she arranged her features into a calm veneer, of course—could have set him ablaze, it was so scorching.

Damn, but he could make a mess of things without even trying. He would be single his entire life if he did not learn how to navigate the waters surrounding women. To be fair, he was not generally addlebrained at the dining table. Somehow he had let the words tumble straight from his mind to his mouth. Now, he would pay the price.

Startling how a woman had the capacity to change from scorching glare to icy stare in a heartbeat.

Miranda lifted her soup spoon and took a taste of what had just been placed before them. The aroma was pleasing, and even without glancing down at his bowl, he identified the soup by its spiciness. One of Nick's favorites, something he had tasted while in Italy, called minestrone. A vegetable soup that was served nearly every time the duke and his wife were visiting.

He waited while she swallowed. Placed her spoon down. Dabbed her lips.

Finally, she turned to him. "I have no idea where Amy is. No inkling what she is thinking. Not a clue what she plans to do. I imagine that takes care of all your questions." She lifted her spoon, stirred the soup and contemplated the vegetables swirling in the broth for a long moment. Without looking up, she added, "I do suspect you have been much, ah, closer to my sister recently than I have. It is a surprise you are not the one to know her schedule."

There was little for him to say.

Oliver took to his soup with more enthusiasm than he felt. Being cut down by the one woman who had chased him his whole adult life was enough to startle him into silence. He deserved what he got, and it was abundantly clear Miranda no longer had any interest in chasing him anywhere.

When his mother engaged his dining partner in conversation, he nearly jumped for joy. He could think of nothing more to say to the woman beside him. The possibility he might put his foot in it again was enough to silence him.

It was an unfortunate turn of events but not without its silver lining. If Miranda no longer desired a match with him, he did not need to be constantly on his guard to keep his distance from her. It was tiring, running from someone who very often lived within his walls.

He turned to Nick, who was smiling at Lucie. How

he would feel blessed if a woman—a certain woman—smiled at him so lovingly. It did not seem likely, since he had apparently upset both sisters in one day. A new record, he thought with a frown.

Interrupting them seemed unkind, but he hadn't had a chance to speak with Nick earlier.

"You do seem to be feeling much better. It is good to see you looking so hale." He tasted his soup. It was divine, another example of the kitchen's prowess. "And I am glad you gave the cook instructions on how to make this. I must admit, it has become one of my favorites."

Nick had already finished, and his bowl had been cleared away. "You have good taste."

"In some things, perhaps. Food being one of them," Oliver allowed. "Other things? Not really."

"Ah, a problem?" His sister's lilting tease made him smile. She was so much more vibrant now that she was married, so much surer of herself. It warmed his heart to see how love had made a difference in her life.

"Not a problem. I just am not as talented as your husband at spreading cheer. I don't know of any wonderful recipes to share, and I am less likely to make a woman smile than frown." He put his spoon down. Gave her a long, appraising look. Goodness, but she was a changed woman. "How does he do it? How does your husband keep that smile on your pretty face? I need to know his secret, if you don't mind sharing."

She leaned closer to Nick, placed a hand on his arm, and gave him a fast wink. The role of wife suited her so well, and it was clear that she was comfortable in it.

"I don't mind sharing, not at all. Although there

really isn't a big secret to it." She paused, then met Nick's gaze with an endearing look in her eyes. Her voice dropped, and she said, "It is love, plain and simple, that brings happiness and laughter. No secret…just love."

Well that was no help at all, was it?

"So that is what I am doing wrong, then. I just need to…ah, well, I don't know—doesn't the whole love thing require emotion on both sides?" He was pretty sure he had finally found his way to the emotion, but by the behavior of the other party, he wasn't sure it was reciprocal. Oh, the complexity of even the basic elements of life were enough to make a man consider celibacy.

He realized the chatter at the table had died somewhat. It occurred to him that Miranda, who so recently had dressed him down, listened in.

There was no keeping the subject quiet now. Once begun, a topic grew a life of its own.

Nick nodded, after a tender glance at his wife. She still had a hand on his arm, so he placed one of his over hers. It all looked very cozy. And, it made Oliver the tiniest bit jealous.

"Why, that does help." He patted Lucie's hand. "Although I can say that even if the other party does not immediately 'fall in love' as the saying goes, it is an emotional state that evolves. Just as love grows deeper with time and circumstance, it also blooms when given the right conditions."

"Sounds rather like a greenhouse orchid." Lord Gregory's observation brought a round of laughter at the table. "Might as well hope for a green thumb as a full heart, it seems."

"Yes, it does at that, doesn't it?" Nick looked at his wife, totally at ease with allowing his admiration to shine for all to witness. "I rather believe my orchid is the loveliest in any greenhouse…"

Lucie's cheeks grew pink.

"Well, yes…" Father sputtered a bit; he was a tad disconcerted with open displays of affection—unless he was the one displaying, in which case it was less discomforting for him. "Ah, right, here we are. The main course. I do hope it is more than the rabbit food old Fairweather has kept me to. I am a bit tired of carrots and cauliflower, my dear."

The doctor, along with the prohibition regarding pipe smoking, ruled out fatty foods. That left a diet of vegetables, fruit and fish, which was good for a man's heart condition but bad for the disposition.

With a long-suffering sigh, purely for the entertainment of all assembled, his wife waved a hand through the air. She turned to the maid who served the vegetables and said, "His Lordship would like an extra-large serving of Brussels sprouts, if you please."

The maid obliged, much to the lord's consternation. But before he could object, his wife turned to the maid holding the next serving plate. "An extra-large serving of the salmon, as well. It is His Lordship's favorite."

"Well…ahem, ah, yes, that is fine."

"Yes, dear, it is very fine." Lady Gregory turned to the man beside her with a gentle smile.

Oliver concealed his amusement. Seated with three couples, at various stages in their marriages, was an education. Perhaps one day in the not too distant future he would put what he was learning into practice.

When they had all been served, they ate in silence for a bit. The sounds of flatware touching china and glassware being placed onto the table after each sip left much room in one's mind for roaming. Oliver wanted to strike a conversation with Miranda, just to make amends for his boorish behavior, but he had no idea what topic might be the safest to broach. Perhaps better to remain silent than further irritate the woman. She hadn't favored him at all during the meal, not even when his elbow grazed hers. That, at another time, would have brought a bloom to her cheeks. Tonight her cheeks were impervious to his touch.

All for the best. His mind was on her sister, there was no question about it. He hated having put Amy off this afternoon. The whole day had been a series of highs and lows, from worrying where she had gone, to searching for her, then finding her. And ultimately, the kiss.

*The kiss.* His heart flopped beneath his evening clothes. Had anyone cared to listen, he was sure it beat loudly enough that it could be heard by another.

But as wonderful as the kiss had been, the aftermath was succinctly the opposite. He had a penchant for making women scowl, it seemed. Especially the Spencer ladies.

Wait. He considered the scowling women. The only ones adversely affected were the Spencer sisters. No one had ever before gone cold on him the way they had done. Whatever could it be, the effect he had on them? If he could uncover what had gone wrong, he would take note and not do the same again.

His mother addressed her question to his sister, and he would not have paid any consideration ordinarily, given the subject matter, but he came to attention.

"Any news of your maid's sister? I am hoping she has not run into some kind of trouble."

"None, Mother. I asked my Abigail, but she did not enlighten me. It is a mystery, and I, like yourself, pray Bridget has not gone down an unhappy path."

"Mother said her leaving was abrupt." Oliver looked for confirmation, and perhaps a bit more of the story, but Lucie just nodded.

"Yes, it was."

"Do you think she has gone…" He left the sentence dangling, the implication clear enough that the words need not be said. If the young woman had taken an unfortunate turn or made a poor decision, it would explain her absence.

Miranda had hardly spoken, but she cut the silence. Putting her knife and fork on the edge of her dinner plate, she dabbed her mouth with her napkin before dropping it onto the table.

"I will never know why a man assumes the worst of a woman whenever he can." She stood, so every man, aside from Nick, stood as well. Miranda turned to his mother, who gazed up at the woman with wide-eyed surprise. "Please excuse me. I feel a headache coming on, and need to lie down."

"Of course, my dear. I shall have some tea sent to your room." Lady Gregory accepted the explanation with good grace, as was her nature.

Miranda turned to the rest of the table, avoiding Oliver's gaze as if to look at him would turn her to stone. She gave a hurried apology, then turned and walked out.

No one said anything for a moment. The men all

returned to their seats as the three women gave each other silent communication. Forks resumed moving on plates and the meal was consumed, but Miranda's leave-taking had left its mark on the party.

The meal was, as were all their meals, tasty, but he did not savor the food. He ate, almost without conscious effort. When he was spoken to, he responded. When desert was over, he, like Miranda, asked to be excused early. If that brought any exchanged, surprised, silent communication between the others, he did not notice. And, he did not care.

The day could have been one of the best of his life. It had some fairly bumpy patches, as well. It was, he decided, time to put an end to it. Tomorrow was a new day, and he sincerely hoped it would have a more consistent flow. Ups and downs put him in a bad mood…a very bad mood.

## Chapter 26

Per Oliver's instructions, the carriage carrying Amy, Miranda, and Vivian had been followed by a second one filled with men from the estate. They did not reveal the truth, but they carried weapons. And, because they did not wish to appear ungrateful, the women did not let on that they were aware of the men's arming themselves.

It was a suitable arrangement for all. It had to be. Only by agreeing to the guards following them had the ladies been granted the use of the carriage they took to Town. Had they balked, it was clear they would remain within the manor's confines.

The ride had been uneventful. When they alighted, accompanied by two maids, they went straight to the millinery shop. It was a favorite of Vivian's, and the other two did not mind. A lady could always find room for one more hat in her closet, so no one objected to the bit of shopping.

Amy was relieved to be free of the estate. The air away from Willowbrook Manor was sweeter somehow. It was all her imagination, but the weight on her shoulders dropped off, about halfway into the trip. It had not returned, so her step was lighter than it had been since she had last seen the man who had done her such a wrong turn.

She and Vivian had not mentioned what she

divulged yesterday, although her friend did pat her hand sympathetically a time or two on the trip into Town.

Miranda was in a foul mood, but she chose to ignore her sister's disposition. Another time, she would have wheedled and cajoled, pulled the truth of what had her in a blue study, but the past weeks had taken their toll on Amy's capacity to shoulder another's worries. She could not help her sister, whatever the reason for her sourness, so why poke and prod until she learned the truth? It did not matter—as so many things that once felt immensely important no longer mattered.

All that was important was this moment, this shopping expedition and taking whatever morsel of fun they could find. She had learned not to count on the future, but to enjoy the present.

As much as one could, that was. Wondering where one man was and what kept him busy was enough of a chore. Wondering about two men nearly addled her brain.

So she forgot about them, for the next few hours at least.

"Exeter's has the nicest straw hats, I think." Vivian stopped to admire the display in the wide window. "Now that is something to think about, isn't it?"

A selection of lace-trimmed creations sat upon a row of faceless burlap "heads" which, when examined closely, all looked strikingly similar. Only the colors were different; the design was identical for all eight.

Amy thought it intriguing. "It is unusual to display the same hat over and over, isn't it?"

"It draws the eye not to the shape of the hat, but to the possibilities each color brings." Vivian nodded appreciatively. Her past endeavors as a seamstress in

Stropshire gave her insight into the business side of fashion neither Amy nor Miranda possessed. "If they were all differently shaped, it would detract from the color selections. It is more a matter now of just deciding which shade goes with an outfit."

"I see…it's not a matter of which hat, but what color." Amy liked the way the other woman saw the reasoning behind the display and was able to pass on her knowledge. She was going to be a good mother when the time came. Not everyone had the talent of being able to explain something so quickly to another.

"Yes, that's it exactly."

Miranda had remained silent. If Vivian noticed the other's sullen nature, she, too, chose to ignore it.

"Shall we go in?" Vivian asked.

"Of course. Why, we are on a lark." Amy smiled at the other's obvious joy. "What kind of lark would this be without at least one hat—each—going home with us? What colors should we choose? Now, that is the question…"

They went inside, where the display was replicated on a side table. Looking glasses were set out in several places so there was no need to crowd in an effort to admire oneself. Vivian and Amy removed their bonnets, setting them out of the way on an empty chair. There was only one other patron in the shop, so when Miranda did not immediately appear beside them Amy turned and found her easily.

Her sister stood gazing into a looking glass. She had not removed her hat, nor had any of the shop's creations in hand. Not vain by nature, Miranda's intense stare at her own face was more startling than the unusual shop window display had been. She had no idea what the other was thinking, but whatever it was it could not be good. No one had ever frowned at her sister the way her own reflection was doing just now.

Amy crossed the space. When she was not acknowledged, she put a hand on her sibling's shoulder. A gentle shake brought a response. Their gazes connected in the looking glass.

"Are you unwell, sister? You have been so quiet all morning. And now…"

"Now? Am I not worthy of admiration? Even if it only myself who is admiring—why, that is what you are thinking, isn't it? I am not comely enough to be appreciated at all—not even by myself!" Miranda's voice was not the calm, low tone that was her habit, but a somewhat louder pitch which was shocking. Amy took her hand away as if burned by the other's accusations.

"How can you say such a thing? Truly, you must be unwell."

"Unwell? As well as unbecoming? Well, you are certainly fashioning a lengthy list of my shortcomings." Her eyes were wild, and her color high. Amy wondered if she had a fever.

"I think we had better get you home. I don't believe you are quite yourself."

Their maids waited outside on the street. They had been talking quietly, but their attention had been turned to the scene inside the shop. The only other shopper, as well as the proprietress, openly stared.

Amy was aware all attention focused on them. Vivian appeared on the other side of Miranda and put a calming arm around her shoulders.

"My dear, are you feeling yourself? We do not

have to shop, you know. We can all go back home directly if you do not feel up to being here."

For an instant Amy feared her sister might lash out at their friend, but she did not. A ragged breath, almost hitched as if it were taxing to inhale, then a weak smile for Vivian.

"No need for that." Miranda took another deep breath, then released it slowly. "I-I suppose I just need some air. If you will excuse me—"

"No—we will go with you." Amy turned to retrieve their hats, but her sister's words stopped her cold.

"I do not wish anyone to go with me. Don't you understand I want to be alone for a while? Not everyone is as enchanted with your company as—well, I am not in the mood to spend the day following you around, admiring your jolly ways and listening to you laugh over every silly thing that catches your fancy." She looked at Vivian, and finished, "I am sorry, Vivian. I just need some time to myself."

Miranda turned and was out the door before anyone could say a word. The stunned silence remained unbroken after she had disappeared around the corner.

Vivian was the first to come to her senses. She put her arms around Amy and pulled her into a tight hug. Her knees were so wobbly, she went willingly and let the other comfort her. How could Miranda have been so horrid? In all their years, she had never once been so hateful.

Rubbing a soothing hand across her back, Vivian murmured, "Pay no attention. She is not angry with you. No, there is something more going on in her head. It is up to us, we who love her most, to determine the cause of her unhappiness and help her out of this sour mood."

"I am the cause of her unhappiness, I think." She stood back and crossed her arms over her chest. The other women had resumed their consultation and were no longer staring. "It is apparent she is angry with me, although I do not understand what I have done to enrage her."

"We all have our moods. Don't take it so much to heart. I am sure she will come around, and apologize. Now, why don't we choose a hat for Miranda? That will make her feel better, don't you think?"

Blue was Miranda's signature color so the choice would take no thought at all. Her heart was not in the gesture, but she did not want to seem as unkind as her sister had been so she agreed. It was terrible enough that one Spencer had displayed her nature so deplorably.

The joy she had so recently felt was gone. She would carry on for Vivian's sake, but the weight was heavy on her shoulders again. Surviving a traitorous heart was a trial under the best of circumstances. When all seemed lost and those closest behaved badly? The challenge was growing and while she smiled and tried on the hat Vivian handed her, she doubted she would survive the ordeals thrown in her way. How could she? Alone and in such an indelicate position?

There is no way out of this bumblebroth. All is lost, she thought.

With a leaden heart, she tied the hat ribbons beneath her chin. It would have suited her just as well had the grosgrain been the hangman's noose. It was how it felt, so why not just have it done with?

## Chapter 27

By the time they got back to Willowbrook Manor, Vivian and the maids were exhausted and worried beyond measure. Amy, however, was furious. Not only with her sister, but with herself. How could she be such an insensitive person? How could she have let Miranda dash off that way?

Their parents hadn't cared for them so they learned early to care for each other. They had always been there, one for the other, always loving, encouraging and relying upon themselves. Letting Miranda leave on her own hadn't been a caring, sisterly action. She had not held her part of their lifelong bargain to support each other, always.

Their bond had begun to unravel when Amy allowed Lyle to position himself in her life so prominently that she pushed her sister to the side. She had put a man—a heartless, self-centered, lying man who did not deserve a mouthful of spit if he were somehow set on fire—more solidly in her heart, mind, and actions than her own flesh and blood. The blame for the way their relationship fell apart was squarely on her shoulders.

"She will be here, certainly." Vivian handed her hat and gloves to one of the maids at the door. "She must have come directly home. I am sure of it, there is no other explanation."

She wasn't at all sure her sister would be at the manor. She had allowed the other woman to repeat the sentiment, time and again, in the carriage, but in her heart she knew better. Miranda was not at the estate.

If bad fortune befalls her, I will never forgive myself, Amy thought as she pulled off her hat and tore her gloves from her fingers. The latter she tossed behind her, not caring at all whether they were caught or crushed underfoot.

They went straight to the front parlor.

A cozy sight greeted them. Lord and Lady Gregory, both reading by the hearth. A low fire burned in the grate, scenting the air with apple wood. Lucie and Nick were not about, but Will and Oliver played whist by the window at the card table. By each man's elbow, a tea cup.

Vivian went straight to her husband. The men all stood when they burst in so she did not stop until she was in his arms.

"Miranda? She is here, isn't she?" Vivian had contained her fear, for Amy's sake, of course, but now that they were back at the estate she did not hold back. Her voice wobbled. "Oh, Will, say she is here, please!"

Oliver crossed the room. Amy had not been able to move from the doorway, so he met her there.

Vivian was pushed gently into the chair Oliver had just vacated by her husband. He knelt before her, taking her hands in his own.

"She is not here, dearest. You took her with you to Town, remember? The three of you went together." Will looked from Vivian, to Amy, then back to his wife. "Miranda is not with you?"

Vivian collapsed in his arms, sobbing against his

chest.

When she would have turned and run from the room, Oliver grabbed her upper arm. Amy could not stand to be held captive, so she tried to shake his hand off, but he held tightly.

"What happened? Tell me, please."

The tone was all business, so she responded in kind. No hysterical outbursts, at least not in public. Later, she might go to pieces, but not in front of everyone. Leave that to the mother-to-be, who was sniffling as she spoke with Will in tones that were hushed but urgent.

"Miranda left." She searched for an explanation that would get her released quickly. Finding her sister was more important than chatter. Right now Oliver's touch, so firm and strong, had to be ignored. She could never, ever fall into a man's web again and lose sight of the only person who loved her enough to endure their rotten childhood by her side. "Please, let me go. I must find her."

Oliver turned, looked back to where Will held his wife against his shoulder. The distress could not be good for the baby. He swept his gaze over his parents, whose shocked expressions and sudden paleness showed they had heard the news.

"I will have the horses saddled. And, order a carriage of men to follow us." He stared into her eyes, and she knew he would expect the truth in a matter of minutes. "We shall find Miranda and bring her home. Do not fret. Just tell me what happened."

Riding came more naturally to her than dancing did, so she tossed her head and said, "I shall explain as we ride. I am going with you."

When he opened his mouth to deny her, she cut him off. Pulling her arm free from his hand, she glared and practically hissed like an angry cat. "I am going, with or without you, to find my sister. I am not your wife; you cannot order me around. I am no man's, and I do as I please. Is that clear, Your Lordship?"

She did not attempt to hide the sarcasm that flavored the formal address.

In that moment, she had no desire to become attached to any man again. The harm her last romantic entanglement had wrought was almost killing her with worry. Even as her heart beat hard in her chest, and her mind screamed to throw herself against Oliver and allow him to comfort her, she could not. It was for the love—or what she thought had been love but was just a cruel joke—of a man that she had sacrificed her own sister. It would never happen again. Never.

"It is perfectly clear." He did not retaliate with sarcasm or take time to reproach her. Instead, Oliver nodded toward the door with a resigned sigh. "Shall we?"

\*\*\*\*

They were nearly to Town. and he had yet to discover the truth of what had happened. Amy rode better than any woman he knew and kept her horse nose to nose with his. They rode hard, which discouraged speech. It was kinder to let her get her wits together. While she pretended to be unaffected by Miranda's disappearance, he knew that was not true.

If ever a sister needed another, it was the case with the Spencer sisters. He could not imagine one without the other. They were not a lot alike, but they were two parts of one whole. They had weathered the storm that was their life when others would have been defeated by circumstance.

It was imperative they find Miranda. To do so, Amy would have to confide in him, whether it pleased her to do so or not.

A rider had gone ahead, so a pair of groomsmen waited their arrival at the townhouse. The horses would be stabled nearby. A fresh pair waited for them, if they were needed. The Gregory stable kept a portion of the larger local establishment for its own use and had animals at the ready at all times.

He dismounted and tossed the reins, knowing they would be caught before they hit the cobblestones. He went to help Amy, who looked ready to fly off her mount on her own. He reached up, put his hands around her slender waist, and lifted her down to the street. She was flushed, from riding or worry, when she met his gaze.

A sheen of unshed tears made her gold-flecked eyes even more luminous. Fear showed clearly, but there were other emotions as well. All swirling in the stare she gave, all just below the surface of incredible restraint. He wished in that moment that she would cry, and he could hold her close to comfort her. Then, perhaps, she would let her guard down.

There were more feelings within him than he knew what to do with. But all of that would have to wait.

"Let's go inside. A pot of tea—"

She looked around, toward the scene on the street. It was an ordinary day. Pedestrians and carriages moved smoothly, and the sun shone down on them all. "I need to go; I need to find her."

"Where will you go?"

Her face crumpled, and a single tear dripped down one cheek. He thumbed it away, surprised that she was so cool on such a warm day.

"I don't know." It was a near-whisper. Her fear cloaked them. "I have to find her, Oliver. Miranda is all I have—all I have ever had."

He willed himself to remain a gentleman and not pull her into his arms, lest some prying eye might see and damage her reputation. It was hard, but he managed to behave the way he knew he must.

"Let's go inside. We can decide what to do over a cup of tea." He turned her gently toward the front door, which stood wide. Jenkins, the butler, waited on the top step ready to assist. As they climbed the wide brick steps, he added, "It will do us both good, I think, if you confide in me. I cannot help when I do not have the facts, Amy. And whatever is going on is less important than getting your sister home where she belongs. Agreed?"

She paused just outside the door. Looked back once more to the street, with all its happy people conducting their daily activities. Then she met his gaze, showing him the full measure of her fear and sorrow. Had he not been prepared, it would have knocked him backward, the emotions were so intense. But he waited, standing firm because he was resolute in his desire to protect those he loved.

And, just looking at the woman before him, his heart swelled. This was more than a friendly connection. His heart was no longer his own.

A small nod. "Agreed."

Chapter 28

"What has been going on with all of you women? I have watched and waited for it to sort itself out—we all have, but it does not seem to be getting sorted."

They were in his office, where walls of books made the place his favorite room in the house. A large walnut desk sat in one corner, with his big brown leather chair behind it, and was the perfect spot for going over accounts or tending to correspondence. Since his return to health, he had taken over most of the family's business, leaving his father free of the burdensome part of their societal responsibilities.

A cluster of high-backed, upholstered chairs gathered around a low table by the fireplace. There was no fire in the grate, but the long shutters were open, and sunlight warmed the room. They sat in a circle of light, his chair pulled so close to hers he could see her bosom moving as she breathed. He pulled his gaze to her face and forced his mind to concentrate on the topic at hand.

"Well?" She did not answer, not even after she took a sip of the Earl Grey. Her cup and saucer landed carefully on the table before she put her hands in her lap and stared stubbornly at the patterned rug at their feet.

Oliver placed his cup beside hers. Leaning forward, he put his elbows on his knees and clasped his hands loosely between his legs. It was, he hoped, a pose to inspire trust.

"Why can't you confide in me? We all know there is something going on, we just do not have any idea what that something might be."

"Who is the all you speak of?"

"Father. Myself. Will. Not Nick; he has too much on his mind already to see how the ladies of the manor are behaving." He spread his hands wide. "If you would enlighten me, I am sure I can help."

"And how exactly are we behaving?" She spoke without taking her gaze from the rug. Its swirls and pattern seemed more interesting than their conversation. "Perhaps you could enlighten me."

He did not take offense at the thin sarcasm. She was under a great deal of pressure, and it was not awful that she showed her human nature.

"You are all acting like a bunch of hens, guarding secrets as if they were eggs and leaving those who care for you in the dark. Pray tell, what is going on?"

It struck him that comparing ladies to barnyard fowl was not the smartest move.

It did not impress Amy, either.

She turned to him, finally, with a horrified, wide-eyed glare. "Did you actually call us chickens?"

"No, of course not." His mind raced. How to get out of the corner he'd painted himself into? "I just feel that I have no idea what is happening in my own household."

Amy scrunched up her nose, as if a vile odor permeated the room. The air was redolent of the scent of lilacs, the vases having been filled for their arrival from the bushes along the back lawn.

"What do you think is happening? With the

chickens you house, I mean."

"I did not call you chickens."

"You did—but go on, please. There must be more, since you seem so wholly unnerved by the women around you." Her eyes flashed, and he could not understand why she was thusly angered. The chicken comparison was harmless. Why was she taking on so?

It was a waste of time, this bickering, but she sat resolute. No help would come from her lips until they worked this out. Better to reason with her than fight her. Men had more muscle, but women were the stronger sex—even if no one readily admitted that.

"Vivian is of course, and understandably so, rather emotional. She is in a state that is accompanied by such mood fluctuations. The doctor told Will to expect…ah, well, to give her temperament some leniency."

She stared in stony silence. So, he went on.

"You have been ill, and I think that is the reason you are so…"

"So what?" Her brow furrowed.

"Well, you are understandably unwell, and it makes you a bit moody. Anyone would be feeling out of sorts if their belly rebelled at every turn." When she did not bite his head off, he stuck his neck out a tad further. "I am concerned by your illness. And, by your refusal to allow Doctor Fairweather to help you. Don't you understand? How you feel matters to us. It matters to me. Please, when we get back to the estate, allow the doctor to examine you. He can help."

Amy pulled a huge breath into her lungs and held it while she turned her gaze back to the rug.

"Can't you just agree to see the doctor?"

She shook her head. It was a small, sad movement

and tore at his heart.

"Why not? He can help you."

Meeting his gaze, she shook her head a second time. "No, he cannot."

Terror shot through him. He fought to keep his voice steady.

"Whatever do you mean? Are you ill—tell me, please, do not keep me in the dark. Are you ill in a dangerous way? Tell me, please."

He was begging, but he did not care. It had so recently come to him that he cared for the woman that the thought she might be deadly ill nearly cut him in pieces. Small, jagged, painful pieces.

"Only dangerous to me, I am afraid."

"I can help, if you will only confide in me. Damn it, Amy, I-I—damn it."

She gave him a shocked grin. "I believe you have already said that. The damn it part, I mean."

"You have to let me help. Don't you understand how I feel about you? Please, don't close me out. If something is wrong, I need to know."

Her hands lay in her lap, and he did not care that it was improper. He took one in his own, and when she tried to pull away, he gentled his touch and ran a fingertip across her palm. Amy ceased resisting, so he spoke softly so she leaned closer to hear. "This is not the time to say what I need to say to you. I am aware of that. But my feelings for you are more than…" He took a deep breath. Time was getting away from them, but he selfishly stole another moment. "I care about you, and when you are unwell, I am unwell. And, if there is a large problem to be solved, it is my hope that you will let me solve it with you. Please, don't shut me out. I cannot stand the thought that something is wrong, yet you won't tell me what it is. Worse still, that you won't accept my help."

She disengaged her hand, but so slowly it seemed she truly did not want to break the connection. He did not force her and twined his fingers together when she placed both hands back on her lap.

"You are sweet, Oliver." The pause was punctuated by a deep breath, then a shaky exhale. "I am grateful, but you cannot help me. It is not something...ahem...well, it is not something that can be undone. No one can help me. Not even you, I am afraid."

He had to know. It would gnaw at him like a flea on a dog unless he asked.

"So you are saying you do not care for me the way I do for you? Is that what you are telling me?"

Amy met his gaze. Her eyes were veiled, and she hid her feelings behind a face whose features were so noncommittal she could have been asked if she preferred Earl Grey to Oolong.

"It is. I do not care for you in that way, Oliver."

His gut told him otherwise, so he was stubborn in his acceptance. "But our kiss? Not to be indelicate, but you kissed me back."

She shrugged. "I was shocked by your behavior. You practically ravished me on the side lawn. What could I do? I was fearful for my life—you are a man, and I am outmatched. What else would any woman do? Can't we leave the unpleasantness behind us?"

Unpleasantness? Good Lord, but could she have lost her mind? Between the nausea and shock of Miranda's absence, perhaps Amy had a case of the mental vapors.

The only other explanation…

"Are you imbibing on a regular basis?"

She stood so quickly her knee knocked the edge of the table. Their cups clinked against their saucers, but neither looked down.

"How dare you?" Amy paled at his accusation. Bright red spots appeared on her cheeks, looking even more impressive against the alabaster tone her skin had turned. "I-I—why, I am appalled by your inference. How dare you—just, how dare you?"

With every 'how dare you' her voice rose. Soon the help would be outside the door, thinking there was something murderous taking place in the room.

"Calm down, please. I did not—"

"How dare you tell me to calm down?"

She stomped a foot. Her hands had found her hips and were fisted on them, pulling her traveling gown upward slightly. He caught a glimpse of her leather boot landing just an inch from his own.

"Amy, really…I do not believe you're thinking rationally. If you would just listen—"

Of course, he had gotten to his feet when she stood.

Now, she pushed past him, a blue-skirted dervish in high temper. As she did, her skirts knocked the table, and their cups and saucers flew in all directions. The sound of shattering china and the scent of spilled cream followed her as she stalked across the room.

"Whatever are you doing?" He was close on her heels, mindful of her toes and tempted to grab her and make her see reason.

He had been irrational many, many times—for many months—while in the throes of addiction. It pained him to believe her capable of such behavior, but anything was possible. He could not cast a dubious eye on anyone after what he had done.

She grabbed the door latch and would have pulled had he not covered her hand and held tight. "Let go—damn it, let go of me!"

He did not immediately release her. There was a fine line between strong handing someone and just trying to protect them from themselves, and he stayed conscious of not being overly forceful. Still, she was not behaving rationally. He could not in good conscience just let her storm out.

"Talk with me, please." He put his mouth close to her ear and spoke quietly. She was so loud that he just wanted her to still. "Amy, I love you. I cannot let you—"

She whirled and faced him. Her eyes were pain-filled, and tears hung on her lower lashes. When she spoke, her anger startled him.

"You do not love me—you are like every other man, talking about love and romance, and-and-and forever—but you don't mean it. It is a ruse, all of it. You-you men, you are all liars in topcoats, not to be trusted." Her tears fell, streaming down her cheeks.

He was dumbstruck by the intensity of her hatred for him.

She scrubbed a hand over a cheek, a sad motion that made his heart fall. He took a step back and broke contact with both her hand and the door latch. Her distress was severe enough that to add to it by keeping her near him when she so vehemently wished to get away was cruel so he did not do it.

Nothing entered his mind. It was completely blank.

Nothing to soothe or smooth her anguish. He had offered her his heart and had been rebuked. After that, what could a gentleman say?

Chapter 29

Amy could not stop the man from following her. She was not afraid; he was one of the grooms from the manor's stable and had been on her tail ever since she left the townhouse. At first, she had run without thinking. But one can only run blindly for so long before stopping to consider the next course of action.

Miranda had been subdued recently, there was no denying it. Not just with her, but with the others, as well. No one pressed her for an explanation, although now it was apparent that someone should have done so.

Who was she trying to fool? She was the person to reach out to her sister, but she had not. Her involvement with Lyle had consumed her, made her self-centered and let her neglect those who mattered most in her life.

What had she done?

London teemed with its usual late afternoon activity. How to find someone who does not wish to be found?

Miranda was a practical person. She did little, if anything, on a whim. Her disappearance had been planned.

On the slim chance that it had been an actual, honest-to-goodness lapse of judgment, she returned to the milliner's. It was, thankfully, empty of shoppers.

The clerk did not look surprised to see her a second time in one day. She smiled, as if it were the norm for three women to behave as they had. Amy appreciated her discretion.

"Hello again." She gave her a big smile, hoping to gain some confidence. "I was in earlier. With my, ah, sisters." A small faradiddle could not hurt. And Vivian was part of the family that she considered her own, so really, how much of a falsehood was it?

"Yes, of course. You purchased three hats; all straw with different color embellishments. One violet, for the lady with the beautiful violet eyes. Yours was green, a deep emerald green that is a particular favorite of mine. And your other sister, the lady who left suddenly? I pray she likes the periwinkle blue, for it matches exactly the lovely outfit she wore."

The woman had keen observation skills. It would be to Amy's advantage if there was a tidbit in that mind which would help her.

"You are a clever woman, indeed. How you recall so vividly what each customer chooses is beyond me, but I commend you for that talent. I, sadly, can barely remember where I last left my reticule."

She attempted to appear cork-brained. In the past, her silly choices had brought the accusation upon her head, usually from Miranda's lips or even Lucie's well-intentioned concern, but the reality was her upper works were just fine.

No one could say that looking for love was a terrible thing to do. It was all she ever wanted. It was what she believed Lyle was offering.

The thought of the man came to mind, but she pushed it aside. He broke her heart, disillusioned her, and shattered her dreams, but it was all for the best. She knew now that she did not love him, and recalling his actions brought a sour taste to her tongue.

Dear God, I hope I am not going to be ill.

She swallowed hard, wishing the wave of biliousness to subside. It did, a little, so she hurried to conclude the visit. Best not to press her luck where her indiscretion was concerned.

"Have you left your reticule?"

The clerk looked about her, checking the shop tables and hat stands with a fast eye.

"No, no…" Amy raised her arm and showed the bag dangling from her wrist. "I have it—today—but there are many instances where I cannot find it. I simply do not have a memory as sublime as yours."

"That is very kind of you to say." The clerk smoothed a hand over her head, patted her white cap where it sat on her modestly styled hair. Hers was a drab outfit and unassertive appearance, the way most clerks presented themselves. Not lessening the beauty and color of the goods they sold, they diminished themselves instead. "Now, what may I do for you? Another bonnet, perhaps? You would look lovely in something in salmon, I think. Such an underappreciated color, salmon."

Just the idea of a salmon-colored hat made Amy's stomach take a turn. Any woman who could carry such a difficult shade without looking nearly-washed out was an exception rather than a rule. It was a horrid color, and everyone knew it was grossly unsuitable for nearly every complexion. Including hers.

Nonetheless, she smiled and accepted the compliment. "Thank you, but no. I do not require another hat today. Perhaps next week, and at that time we should revisit the notion of some, ah, salmon embellishments." Her tummy lurched as she forced the word through tight lips.

"I will look forward to that meeting."

"As will I." She swallowed again, feeling too warm inside the shop. Its wide windows let sunlight fill the space. Good for inspecting feathers and ribbons, but awful for the constitution. She hurried on. "I wonder if you saw my sister a second time. I mean, after we left…did she return?"

"The one with the lavender eyes?"

Time sped by, and she still had no idea where Miranda had gone. Impatience made her tone sharp. "No, not that one."

The clerk's mouth opened in surprise. She did not try to stall or share more shop talk. She nodded, and said, "The sister in blue? Yes, she was here. She returned just after you left."

Amy wanted to climb over the display table separating them and grab the woman. Why hadn't she said that right off?

"What did she say?"

"Nothing. She didn't say a word," the woman insisted, backing away from the table. The extra space between them could not keep her from divulging whatever she knew. Amy would not give up until she learned all she could from the woman whose gaze shot to the open doorway, as if she either looked for escape or prayed for assistance.

"You would have me believe she came in, walked around, and simply left? That makes no sense."

"She came back, but did not shop. Before I could ask if she needed my help, she turned and left. Just walked out—it is the truth, I swear it is."

The clerk's hands twisted together. Her fingertips were reddened from working with wire and straw, and she looked ready to cry. A stab of remorse shot through her, but it wasn't enough to keep her from pushing for answers.

"Which way did she go? When she walked out, which way did she turn?"

A shaking finger pointed the way.

"Right. Toward Bond Street."

\*\*\*\*

Oliver was not above following Amy, but when one of the men he had dispatched from the manor returned with news, he had to make a choice. Following a woman who professed to hate him when he knew she was not willing to listen was a wasted effort. His other option? To go where he knew the missing sister was headed, and await her arrival.

He did not love Miranda in more than a brotherly manner, but he could not allow her to ruin her life. And, if he did not stop her, she would do exactly that.

The ride was not a difficult one, and he knew she was only partway there. The stage would not leave again before morning, so he did not push the horses. Riding without haste gave him time to consider the mess his life had become. It was almost too much to bear, that he had been lost, then found by the beating of his own heart, then lost again because his affection had been spurned. It was enough to make a man consider taking up the drink, but he had done enough of that already to last a lifetime.

The inn at Birmingham bustled with activity. The main stopping point between London and the south of Scotland, it saw visitors passing from one point to the other all day long, and sometimes well into the night.

He walked into the inn, narrowly avoiding being knocked over by a baggage man serving one of the coaches. The poor fellow labored under the weight of no less than five satchels, so Oliver waited for him to pass before he went to the accommodations bar.

"Full up, we are. Can put you in the stable, though, if you like." The man behind the counter looked from black boots to the black hat Oliver wore, a slow smile spreading across his face. He looked the sort to spend evenings in the pub, his eyes bloodshot in the afternoon and his nose and cheeks ruddy from years of whiskey. He coughed, spat onto the floor, and added, "Likely you're not used to such accommodations, but it's all we've got. Busy, as you see."

A fresh wave of baggage passed, this time borne on the backs of two young boys. They were positively bent over with the weight of what they toted.

Oliver watched them pass.

The clerk pointed a twisted finger. "Sons do come in handy, don't they?"

He thought that if he was ever fortunate enough to have sons, he would not mistreat them like the two who disappeared around the corner. Theirs was a difficult life, but to use children as pack mules was near barbarism.

Saying so would do no good. It might even lead to a beating for the boys, if the man were the sort to do that, so Oliver kept his mouth shut on the subject.

He addressed the man with a civil tongue. "I am looking for a woman."

A wink, and a grunt. "Aren't we all?"

"No, you do not understand, I am looking for a

particular woman."

The clerk laughed, showing rows of blackened teeth. "Like I said, aren't we all?" He waved when Oliver opened his mouth to clarify, going on with another wink. "Now, now, I was just having sport with you. Of course, there's more to the place than a bowl of stew, a beer, and a bed. I can get you a woman. For a price, you understand."

His stomach turned. What a world they lived in. Children mistreated. Women bought and sold. So much wrong with what they deemed socially acceptable.

He couldn't change any of that. But he could keep one young woman from making a terrible mistake. That had to be enough.

"The woman I wish to see has arrived on the coach two hours ago. I presume she is in an upstairs room, refreshing herself after the arduous trip." He put his hand in his trouser pocket. The man's gaze followed, narrowing suspiciously when Oliver did not pull it out right away.

"A lot of women are upstairs."

"Not all arrived on the two o'clock coach from London."

The clerk gave a dismissive shake of his head. "There are many women here. Sorry, but I can't help you."

He took his hand from his pocket, letting the Sovereigns jingle in his palm. "I think you can."

Leaning closer, the clerk eyed the money with such greed it made Oliver sick. "What she look like, this woman of yours?"

Chapter 30

Miranda had come without much fuss. In fact, she almost seemed happy to see him. The room she occupied was dark and dreary, and she looked completely lost when she opened the door to him. Frightened, too.

Her eyes had been reddened and were still puffy, so he knew she had shed many tears. She looked as if she had aged since yesterday. Dark circles. Hair, usually done to perfection, drooping where it generally curled. The signature blue traveling dress was wrinkled, its hem muddied along with her boots.

He hated to add to her misery, but there was no way around it. And since they were nearly back to Willowbrook, their time was limited. Better to discuss in private, as there would be enough questions awaiting her from the others.

"Where were you going?" He spoke gently, hoping she would not feel pressed into a corner.

There was no fight left in the woman. She shrugged, a tiny, helpless gesture. He did not feel any desire for her, but he did not wish to see her so dejected.

"You know where."

"Why?"

A snort, so uncharacteristic and unladylike. So out of what he expected, he smiled. Just a small show of amusement for the quick bit of defiance.

For ultimately, a snort was a markedly defiant gesture when coming from a lady.

"Why do women go to Gretna Green?" She sighed. "You know why they visit the blacksmith shop. Why they hand fast. Why they rush to make a match that is probably very unsuitable. You know the answers, Oliver, so please don't be coy."

He ran an exasperated hand through his hair. The day had been a long one, and it was nowhere near over yet.

"I do not understand why you would run off to that place. Were you to meet someone there?"

A second snort, louder than the first. She looked up, met his gaze, and he realized she was a hair's breadth from breaking down. Perhaps a woman could be like a horse, pushed until they gave in. Then, he could help her find her way to contentment. It worked with his livestock, but he had already made a fool of himself comparing one woman to a bird so he kept his thoughts to himself.

"I know you think no man will ever want me so I wish I were the type to spin tales. I would lie, and say I was keeping an assignation with a tall, dark, handsome fellow. I would say we are madly in love, but he is not a peer so we are forced to go to Scotland to fulfill our destinies. I would say he is right this minute wondering where I am, pining for me and holding his breath until he sees my smiling face again. If I were the type to say such things, I would…"

It had come in such a rush he had not been able to get one word in. As soon as she left off, he spoke in earnest.

"Miranda, we need to clear this between us. It has been hanging on for years. It is my fault I have not said a word before now. Forgive me, please."

"Don't say what I think you are going to say. I cannot take it."

"It needs to be said." He chose his words with care. "I admire you greatly. You are a wonderful woman. Brilliant. Witty. An excellent dancer. A lovely dinner partner." When she snorted again, he was going to ignore it but took a chance. "A world-class snorter."

"Oliver—you didn't just say that!"

She did not look ready to cry anymore, so he nodded and gave her a little grin.

"Oh, but I did. Why, I do believe I have never met a woman who snorts half as well as you do."

She giggled. "You know many snorting women, then?"

"Why, loads of them."

Miranda smoothed a hand down the front of her skirt. She seemed to come alive and realize the condition of her clothing. A resigned head shake set a curl bobbing near her cheek. She pushed it back, but it fell forward, too tired to stay where it should.

"I am a mess." She gave an apologetic shrug. "Although I do not need to worry when I am in your company. You do not care for me so it does not matter how I present myself. That is somewhat freeing, I must say."

At least they were talking. Now, to set things straight.

"Miranda, who were you going to meet at Gretna Green?"

She shook her head. "No one. I don't know what I

thought, really. Maybe that there would be all sorts of men ready to marry women who just wanted some…"

A gentle tone, a tiny smile. A bit of encouragement. "Some what?"

She met his gaze with the most honest expression he had seen from her in a long while. It hit him that she no longer looked on him as if he were a piece of cheese and she a hungry mouse. It was a different assessment, one that was friendlier. He liked it.

"Some happiness. That's all anyone wants, isn't it? To be loved. To be happy. To feel life is worth living. To plan for a future." She wiped the tear that rolled down her cheek. "All around me, that is what everyone is doing. Vivian and Will. Lucie and Nick. Amy and Lyle—why, they were so on the high ropes I am sure my own sister does not even remember I am alive. And you…you who does not want me."

"We are more suited to be friends." The truth had to make things better for both of them, but it was damn hard to get past his lips. "We both know I am not inclined to feel the way you did."

She raised one perfectly arched eyebrow. "Did?"

He flashed a conciliatory grin. "Certainly. I know that if you sought other prospects—in Scotland, for instance—you must not be as enamored with a certain silly man we both know."

"Know well," she said softly. "And love."

"As a sister toward a brother. It is not in the stars for us, dear Miranda. We could force the association, but we are so suited to friendship—deep, abiding, lifelong friendship. Don't you agree?"

The carriage turned in the wide estate entrance. They did not have much time left to come to an understanding.

"I do, actually. I am sorry to have put us in such an uncomfortable position all this time, Oliver. I pray you will forgive me. I have grown and believe my infatuation has become something I've gone past. It was not the kind of true love I see Lucie feel for Nick, or Vivian for Will."

A lump filled his throat, making it near impossible to swallow. Harder, still, to speak.

"Amy for Lyle, as well."

Miranda did not hesitate. "No, I don't think that is the case. In fact, I know it is not. She doesn't love him. She thought she did, certainly, but his actions have pushed her aside. He is not a gentleman, not at all."

"I thought she loved him."

"I believe she thought she loved him, also." Miranda shook her head, but not in dismay. "I am glad it did not work out with Lyle Roarke. The man is too full of himself by far. He was not good for my sister, although it took his showing his hand as a full-on rake for her to believe that."

Oliver was stunned. He thought Amy rebuffed his declaration because she loved another. But now…

He paid attention, because now that Miranda had begun, she did not seem inclined to stop chatting. And, she needed no partner, just a captive audience. Which, for the next few minutes at least, he was.

"I want a love like the others have found. I realize we are not a good match, so you needn't be concerned I will attempt to ensnare you. No…I want a love that makes a man swoon when I walk through the door, the way Will and Nick do for their wives. And I want children, the way they do, as well."

It was a delicate conversation to have, but they were alone. He took a leap of faith. She hadn't smacked him yet so his luck might hold out for a bit longer.

"Vivian is, ah, in the family way."

"You are very observant." The comment came with a little grin.

"Lucie?"

Miranda shook her head. "No, but hopefully soon. One of the maids is helping, with a draught to make that happen more easily." She stopped, clapped a hand over her mouth and inhaled sharply. "Oh, no. That was a secret."

She always had been the one, between Amy and Lucie, to let a cat out of a bag. Even as children, she had not been good at keeping secrets.

"It is fine. I will not let on that I know Bridget went to see Old Dorinda. I honestly did not realize she went for Lucie and Nick."

Miranda's hand came off her mouth in an instant. "How do you know all this?"

"I observed the maid on her mission. But, as I say, I did not know the potion was for my sister and Nick."

She waved her hand vigorously in the air between them. Had he not leaned back, she would have hit him in the nose. Unintentionally, but her excitement was such that her aim was poor.

"No—not for Nick. He does not know—and he cannot know. I beg you, don't tell him. She will get with child soon, and we can pretend this conversation did not happen. Please, Oliver, say you will keep my confidence."

His mind swam, filled with thoughts and questions, but he agreed to her request without misgiving. It really was none of his affair how the marital bed was laid. He simply prayed Lucie and Nick would have as many children as they wished, and all healthy and happy.

"I don't know what you speak of, my dear. Not a clue."

"Oh, thank you. Sometimes my mouth gets away from me."

They were nearing the manor so Oliver asked, "What about Amy?"

"What do you mean?"

He hated himself for even wondering, but he had to know.

"Is she also in the family way? Please, now you must tell me. And I promise, I will never speak a word of this conversation to anyone. I have to know, Miranda—is your sister with child?"

She studied him for a long, silent moment. His heart felt trapped in his chest, his anxiousness to know was so sincere.

"You love her, don't you?"

"A question should not be answered with another question."

"Answer me, and I will answer you. You love my sister, don't you?"

There was no way to lie. And if there had been, he still would have told the truth. He hadn't waited his whole life to fall in love with someone only to deny the fact when asked.

"I do. I love her."

"I am sorry, then." Miranda leaned closer, her countenance once again sad. Reaching out a hand, she grasped his and gave a comforting squeeze. "I am not certain, but I do believe my sister has been ruined by that rake. She has been suffering symptoms similar to those Vivian endures, and has been so morose, and wholly unlike herself, that I can think of no other explanation for it."

His heart fell to his knees. It was good they were seated, because he was not sure his legs would hold him upright.

"You think she is having his baby."

"Yes, I do. But I know she will never tell him if that is the case. He hurt her so badly, I do believe she would rather die than spend her life with that horrible man."

Chapter 31

Oliver waited until the next day before he sought out Amy.

He did not want to risk another unpleasant scene with her. They were all worn thin from the day, so he did not go into the library where everyone had assembled. When he departed for Scotland, he had dispatched the messenger to find Amy and the groom who followed her. They brought her home, with the assurance that he would bring her sister home before the night was over.

It was good that they were all back at Willowbrook. But how to keep the peace? So much went with being lord of the manor, things he had never realized, that before he left the breakfast table that morning he thanked Father.

Shock colored the old gentleman's face red. He waved the unlit pipe that was never far from his hand. "Oh, all in the life of a peer, my son. You will find out when I am gone, that running an estate—or two, or three—takes a firm hand. Patience. And—" he gazed at his wife before finishing, "—a loving heart. You will do well when I am gone."

"Thank you for your confidence. I hope I make you proud."

Lady Gregory lifted her cheek when he bent to kiss her. "Get yourself a wife, Oliver. A good woman to help you, someone to share your days and nights with, a loving woman to give you sons and daughters. That is what life is about, really...happiness and family."

Father nodded, the few white curls left on his head bobbing as he did. "Your mother is quite right, son. A wife, that is the ticket."

They were the only ones who appeared for breakfast so he did not hesitate to reply openly.

"It is what I hope to do, sooner rather than later. I am at the point in life where someone to share the joys with sounds like a dream come true. I have not wished to make a match before now, but it is time."

His mother clapped her hands, a smile stretched across her face. She was giddy as a girl at the announcement. As he expected, she did not let him get off with just proclaiming his intention.

When he began to walk away, Mother grabbed his wrist. For a lady getting on in years, her grip was surprisingly firm.

"Who? Please, tell. Why, I couldn't stand the wondering if you do not."

"That is right, son. She would drive me mad trying to puzzle out the rest, so please, if you care one whit about my sanity, tell your mother whatever she wants to know." He stuck the pipe between his teeth and bit down.

"Yes, I shall badger your father night and day until I know the truth." Her grip loosened. She put her hands together, imploring as only a mother can. "So you really think you are ready to make a match?"

"I not only think I am ready...I know I am ready, Mother." He put a hand on one of her shoulders. The other, he put on his father's shoulder. Linked thusly, he added, "I have already chosen a wife. Now, to make her choose me, as well…that is the difficult part, it seems."

His parents exchanged surprised glances.

"Show her how much you love her, and she will not be able to resist your charms. After all, that is what every woman wants, to love and be loved."

His father took the pipe from his mouth and looked at his wife. "It is what everyone wants, my dear. Not just women, but everyone."

Oliver left them smiling at each other and went in search of Amy.

She was where he thought she might be. And, she was alone.

"Do you mind if I join you?"

She looked up from her canvas, but not at him. The glance was for the rosebushes she painted, making them more vibrant in her oils than they were hanging from the vines.

"If you wish." Three cold, clipped words.

He would not be discouraged. A woman in her state had a right to be out of sorts, so he moved her paint box off the chair beside her, placed it on the grass, and sat. They did not speak for many minutes. As he watched, she made the painting come more fully alive. A spot of color, a bit of feathering, and flowers stood out so beautifully he was tempted to lean close and inhale their aroma.

When she could go no further without waiting for the paint to dry, she set aside her palette and brush. She folded her hands in her lap and refused to look at him.

"Amy—"

"Thank you for bringing Miranda back." She spoke as if she rehearsed the words. No emotion, with her hands clasped tightly where they lay. "I am grateful."

"You're welcome." He waited, but when she did not say anything more, he began again. "Amy, we need to discuss some very important things."

"There is nothing to discuss."

Her jaw clenched, and a vein throbbed in her temple. They were the only signs of her duress. He ached to reach over and still the throbbing, unclench the jaw, but knew better than to try. Not yet. She was not ready.

"I think we have much to discuss, if only you will give us a chance."

"Chances are for children. We are adults, and there is nothing for us to talk about."

Amy rose and undid the tie that held her painting smock in place. She removed the smock, crumpled it into a wad and tossed it onto her chair. The canvas was too wet by far to pack up and move, so she stalked off toward the closest rose hedge.

Not an easy nut to crack, he thought. But, he hadn't expected she would fall over at his feet when she saw him.

He left his seat and went to where she stood. The arbor shaded them, and the air was a riot of spicy scents. The rosebushes here were delicate shades of pink. It was where his mother came to read, beneath the pergola.

It was where father had proposed marriage, so many years ago, in the very same spot.

"You cannot be so hardened against me that you will not even speak with me."

He had considered his words all night long, but when it came down to it, there had been no need to rehearse a speech or decipher his feelings. All he had to do was speak from his heart and pray her heart could hear his.

"There is nothing—"

It was impolite, but he did not allow her to finish.

"Yes, I heard that. But you are wrong." The powers of persuasion had to be heartfelt if they were going to make this happen. "There is a great deal to discuss. But first, I need to ask a question, and I pray you will give me an honest answer."

She looked up with frightened eyes.

"You have nothing to fear from me—why do you look like a startled rabbit about to be devoured by a lion? For goodness sake, you know me well enough to know I will never harm you."

"Don't ask any questions. Please, just don't."

"I must. And I will not leave until you answer honestly."

"Honestly? Isn't that a loose term coming from a man?" The hurt in her voice made the words less insulting.

"I am not just any man. And, all men are not the same."

"That is what all men say, Oliver. So, who can believe that?"

He took a deep breath. Fighting would get them nowhere, so he did not push back. The verbal war had to end.

"My question…do you love Lyle Roarke?"

Her eyes rounded in surprise. "Are you mad? Why would you ask such a question?"

Was he mad? At one time, perhaps, but not any longer.

"I need to know. That is reason enough to ask." He paused, studying the beautiful eyes he knew so well for a sign of her affections. There was nothing to indicate the heart of the woman behind the eyes. "I ask again: Do you love Lyle Roarke?"

"No. I do not."

He was so elated, he could have picked her up, whirled her around and kissed her. But, the stormy expression on her face had not gone away, so he hid his relief.

A very restrained nod, when he wished to scream with joy. "That—well, that is good. I am glad to hear you are not in love with him."

"Why?"

"Because I love you. And if you love another…well, it would make things rather difficult."

There. It was out. He had said the words, and so far she had not run off. But, there were no doors here for him to hold closed. If she chose to, she could be lost in the labyrinth of roses faster than the rabbit she had so recently resembled.

Amy's shoulders fell. "Oliver, don't…"

He stepped closer, so close they were nearly nose to nose. This was his one chance, his only chance and he'd be damned if he let it slip away.

"Don't what? Tell you the truth—that I have loved you for so long I cannot recall when my loving you began? That I cannot think of anyone but you—and when I fall asleep at night you are the last person I think of? Or that when I wake in the morning, you are on my mind and in my heart before my eyes are even open? Don't? Can't you see I must?"

He hadn't meant to become so impassioned but it

all came tumbling from his mouth in a rush.

She spun and would have run, but he reached out and caught her in his arms. Turned her to face him, and asked, "Amy? Don't you understand how much I love you?"

"Please, can't you leave me alone?"

She began to cry, but he was quite sure she was not even aware of the tears. They slid down her cheeks and dripped onto her butter yellow morning gown. A tendril of hair escaped her white lace cap, so he swept it off her face with a thumb. He cradled her head in his hand, searched her eyes for an answer. So much pain, in someone so lovely—it was an abomination, this torture.

"I cannot leave you alone. You see, you have my heart, and where one's heart goes, one must also go."

The tears fell more swiftly. "I don't deserve your love."

"How can you say that? Of course you do—and I have loved you without realizing that was the emotion I have been feeling. I am not experienced in this matchmaking business. I am a fool, honestly, for not professing my love to you before it was this late."

She scrubbed a hand over her eyes. They were stunning, even reddened and tear-soaked.

"It is too late." Amy caught her breath and slowed her crying. He watched her take control, saw how she did not allow herself to continue to let the teardrops fall.

"It is never too late," he said softly. "Never."

The breath was long and jagged, but she pulled it in and steadied herself. "It is for me. Find someone else, please."

"There is no one else."

"There has to be." She shook in his arms, and he hated the sadness in her voice. "I'm not good enough for you, don't you understand? I have made mistakes that cannot be undone. I am not—oh, Oliver, I am not who you think I am."

When she pulled loose, he released her. Not because he wanted to let her go, but because he did not want to hold her confined. When she came to him, if she came to him, it had to be out of love, not because he trapped her. But he did not let her get far. When she reached the end of the pergola, he reached for her again.

"Amy, please. This is ridiculous—I swear, I will follow you to the ends of the earth if you force me to do so. And you are wrong; you are who I think you are. It is not your fault that your first affair was with a rake—you could not know."

She whirled to face him. Color drained from her cheeks, and her mouth opened wide. She inhaled sharply, placing a hand on her chest.

"You know?"

He ran a hand through his hair. Suddenly this was not going as he hoped. She looked scandalized, and of course she would, but a man could only dance around the truth for so long without pulling it out into the light of day.

"It does not matter to me, whatever happened between you and him—I do not care, it is not important. It does not change how I feel about you."

She stared at him as if he had gone crazy right before her eyes.

"How can it not? Honestly, it changes how I feel about myself. That a man could treat a woman that way. Use her for his own purposes, then toss her aside—oh,

God, I am ruined—and you say it does not matter? It matters!"

A granite bench ran the length of the pergola. Amy sat, looking as if her legs simply gave out. She put a hand on her face and began to cry.

Dropping to his knees before her, he placed himself so she had no choice but to look at him. Having watched his parents, he knew that marriage was not all roses. It was not always easy. It had its share of messy moments. They did not scare him. And, the time to begin to show that was at the very start.

"What matters is how you are now. This…ah, this matter is only going to get bigger. We need to consult the doctor."

"We?"

He nodded. There was no going back. Whatever had happened, he could not undo. All he had was now, and their futures depended on how they dealt with whatever obstacles stood in their way.

"You are not alone. Amy, I love you. Do you feel even the tiniest bit of emotion for me? Please, don't spare my feelings. I need to know the truth."

She swallowed hard. Wiped a tear from her cheek. Searched his eyes with a long, soulful stare. Quietly, she said, "I am ruined. Do you understand what I am saying?"

It was hard for a man to take, but he hadn't been a choirboy when he'd been lured in by the addiction. He had done some things he would never be proud of, and had seen things he wished he hadn't. Everyone had demons they fought, secrets they carried…he could not fault her for being human.

"I understand. You gave yourself to—"

"No—I did not! I never gave myself to him." Her tone became frantic, her eyes pleading with him to believe her. "He wanted me to, but I couldn't. I thought that if he loved me, he would marry me. And then—well, then I would do what every wife does. But no, I never gave myself to him, I swear to you."

Confusion flashed through his mind, but the flash was ever-so brief. Cold hatred for the man filled him when he realized what she had not been able to say.

"He forced himself on you?"

Amy glanced at his hands. They had curled into fists without any conscious effort. Oliver took a deep breath and relaxed his fingers. She watched, and when he did not appear ready to punch something, nodded.

"I tried to make him stop. He was drunk, after the Farthington Ball, when everyone was walking on the terrace. He pulled me into a side room, in the back hallway. I thought he would steal a kiss, and he was drunk. And I did not want to make a scene, but…" Amy covered her face with her hands and sobbed. He cradled her shaking body against his chest. The storm did not pass quickly, but he held her close. She needed to release the wretchedness she had held inside all these weeks. He thought back; the Farthington Ball had been three weeks prior. It had been since then that she had been ill, not quite herself. It all made sense now.

Roarke would get his due. Eventually. Now, Amy was far more important than that miserable excuse for a man.

When she sniffled, but no longer sobbed, he took his handkerchief from his pocket. He dabbed her eyes, then handed it to her so she could blow her nose. She did, then clutched the white linen in one hand.

"I need to ask…"

She met his gaze. They were close enough to kiss, but it was hardly the time. She did not look away, and he was grateful.

"You want to know what happened. There is not much to tell, really. I hit my head and do not remember—well, I do not remember all of it."

The more he heard, the more furious he became, but he could not let her know that.

"How did you hit your head?"

Amy rubbed a spot on her temple. He reached out, felt it with gentle fingertips. There was a small lump.

It made him see red. Still, he did not let on.

She sighed. "He was drunk, as I said. He wanted— well, he wanted what I would not willingly give, so he pushed me against a wall and…my clothing was ripping, I could hear buttons hitting the floor as they flew off my gown. I remember trying to push him away, but he was strong. The more I pushed, the more he insisted. He tore my bodice, and…" Amy looked down at her hands. "He exposed my breasts. I wanted to scream, but I did not wish everyone to see me that way, so I pushed hard against him. And, I fell. There was a bookcase—my head hit and that was that. When I woke, he was gone."

That bastard! Oliver fought for control. He was nearly out of his mind with rage, yet he could not show the state of his emotion. It would not help Amy, and until she was sorted out, killing the scoundrel would have to wait.

"So you do not remember what he did to you?"

A fast head shake of denial. "I don't. It's all a blur, after I fell. When I woke, I wore a shawl I found in a dresser in the room to cover myself. I came home with the others. I never saw him again. Nor do I want to."

"You need never see that man again, I promise. I must ask, did you seek help for your injuries?"

"My head? No, I just took to my bed for a day or two. I didn't want to speak with anyone after what happened." She looked at him, offering a tight smile. "I didn't have anything to say."

"But your other injuries? Surely, when he violated you—ah…"

"No. No, he did not." Amy colored, but shook her head. "I am sure, he did not. My clothing was intact…ah, it was not disturbed. And, there was no…oh, believe me, he did not do what you are thinking."

Relief washed over him. Not that it would have made a difference in how he felt for her, but it made a difference in how she felt about herself.

"Well that is good news. I hate that he did that to you, and I am sorry I cannot change what has been done." He had been sitting beside her ever since she began to cry. Holding her in his arms, he had no wish to ever let her go. "But you have been so ill. I thought you might be with child."

"No, it is not that." She shrugged. "I am just prone to unfortunate nervousness when I cannot stand something. And being in this situation…well, it has definitely had me at sixes and sevens. I have felt so foolish. But, not in the family way, thankfully."

"Yes, that is more good news. And I pray your nerves will settle, now that you have unburdened yourself."

"Time heals. I am not upset that he is gone. I did

not love him. I tried, but I couldn't. He was not the man for me, and it is good he is out of my life. It is too bad he ruined me, though. I hate that thought."

Oliver's hope lifted.

"No one knows what happened. And, as you said, he did not—well, he was not as brutal as he could have been. I give you my word that you will never again be bothered by that man. Not for the rest of your life. So, why not put it out of your mind, and don't let yourself dwell on what cannot be changed. You are not ruined— you could never be ruined."

Her eyes were less troubled. Her brow had relaxed. And the vein that throbbed in her temple still pulsed, but less stringently. Her body was not as taut in his arms. They were making progress, but there were still hurdles to face.

"You did not answer my question, Amy. I am not in the habit of forgetting the important things in life, and that was one of the most important questions I have ever asked. Have you forgotten? Wait, I shall ask again: I need to know, do you love me at all?"

She released a long, slow breath. When she met his gaze, she flashed a little smile. "I have always had feelings for you. That is why I took up with—well, you know who I mean. I formed an attachment to him because you did not look my way. And, Miranda constantly looked your way. What choice did I have?"

He was learning to follow the female line of thinking, but he was still far from being an expert. She addled his mind, so he held up a hand as he pondered her response.

Had she said what he thought she said?

"Are you saying that you love me?" He had to be

sure. And if she didn't, he had to be sure of that, too.

Amy's eyes were wide. Beautiful. Honest. She looked at him, and Oliver felt his soul melt. It was an experience like no other, and he did not want it to end. Ever.

"I am. I have…always."

His mouth claimed hers. It was a tender kiss that sealed promises, fates and futures. Oliver wished he could kiss her forever, right under the pergola where his parents had proclaimed their love for one another. It was not possible, so he pulled his lips off hers with a groan.

Someday soon they would be free to kiss and kiss and kiss, without regard for propriety or what the kisses would encourage between them. Someday, they would have children.

But, first things first.

Oliver cleared his throat and smiled at the woman in his arms. She smiled back, sending his heart soaring out of his chest. He felt free enough to fly over the estate, like a bird. It was wild. Exhilarating. Joyful.

"Amy, I love you. Please, will you do me the honor of becoming my wife? I promise to be the best husband I can be and to love you every day of my life. Please, say yes."

"Yes."

And with that, their fates were sealed. Beneath the pergola on a warm, sunny morning, they proclaimed their love. Kissed until they were ready to burst with excitement over the prospect of what lay ahead.

Then, he took her hand, and they walked toward the manor. Where, if Oliver guessed correctly, his mother was already planning a celebratory engagement dinner.

As Old Dorinda would say, the stars aligned and the heavens smiled, and love bloomed between a man and a woman when the time was right.

Oliver was grateful that time was now.

## A word about the author...

Sarita Leone loves adventure, whether it be in a distant continent or her own backyard. When she's not off exploring the world, she keeps busy writing, reading, and dancing beneath the stars. Always a fan of happy endings, she's fortunate to have a job which allows for so many of those! She loves to hear from readers. Easiest way to connect? Check out her Facebook page, where all the latest news hits the screen.

Thank you for purchasing
this publication of The Wild Rose Press, Inc.

If you enjoyed the story, we would appreciate your
letting others know by leaving a review.

For other wonderful stories,
please visit our on-line bookstore at
www.thewildrosepress.com.

For questions or more information
contact us at
info@thewildrosepress.com.

The Wild Rose Press, Inc.
www.thewildrosepress.com

Stay current with The Wild Rose Press, Inc.

Like us on Facebook

https://www.facebook.com/TheWildRosePress

And Follow us on Twitter
https://twitter.com/WildRosePress